Nomads Nest, Population: 12
by
Carly Berg

Nomads Nest, Population: 12 is a work of fiction.
Unless otherwise indicated, all the names, characters,
businesses, places, events and incidents in this book are
either the product of the author's imagination or used in
a fictitious manner. Any resemblance to actual persons,
living or dead, or actual events is purely coincidental

Table of Contents

For Angelo, my honey helper.

A Small Dot on the Map

Lonnie sat in the passenger seat of the eighteen-wheeler, imagining herself to be starring in a film. The movie running through her mind featured herself in the role of a young woman who was running away from her entire life. That's precisely what Lonnie was doing but it seemed so surreal that it played like a film in her mind.

She imagined a voice-over narrating the scene as she rode down the highway next to a real life over-the-road trucker whose name was Wayne. The voice said, *One thing you'll remember later, if you ever hitch a ride in an eighteen-wheeler through Wyoming, Montana and up into Canada, is that nobody's there. Practically nobody. Sure, tiny towns dot the landscape, but only here and there, between great uninhabited swaths of mountain and prairie. Riding high through it all, in the cab of a semi, you can see for miles around. And let me tell you, this whole massive chunk of the continent is damn empty.*

Lonnie took a swig of Coke. She lit a cigarette, then inhaled and exhaled dramatically, holding the cigarette up in the air in glamorous, movie star style. Wayne rolled his eyes and rolled his window down. The voice-over continued, *Another thing you'll remember is the sky. Your view of the heavens will be vast, wide open. The big sky's ever-changing show astonishes. White swirling with blue and grey, some days. Other times, lightning like a fireworks display. People say you can see the neon green and purple of the northern lights here on winter nights. And when a storm's approaching, as one is now, well, it's just wildly gorgeous. No seascape in the world outshines these skyscapes.*

Wayne, the trucker, said, "Did you say something, darlin'?"

"No," Lonnie said, startled by the intrusion. She stubbed her cigarette out in the ashtray. Wayne rolled his window back up. The voice resumed: *Meanwhile, down here on the ground in Alberta, we're in desolate prairie country, approaching the village of Nomads Nest, population: 12.*

Wayne cut into Lonnie's reverie again. "Geez, we're in for a heck of a storm. Hope I can get this load to Edmonton ahead of it. First, I've got to refuel, though. My apartment's above that truck stop over there, you know."

He pulled off the highway and into the parking lot of the truck stop, if you could call it that, the old convenience store with a couple of fuel pumps, and a couple of stories on top. By "storm," she guessed he meant a rainstorm, not a snowstorm. Though even now, in mid-April, there were scattered patches of snow on the ground. She said, "You live here? Why? I mean, not that there's anything wrong with it. It just seems so… far from everything."

"Well, geez, it's only an hour from Calgary. But yep, the whole population of Nomads Nest lives in the six apartments above the truck stop. People seem to just blow in off the highway coming up from the states. Then they end up staying a while. I like it, though. It's cheap and it's on my route."

Lonnie said, "I read about a town in Alaska that's sort of like that. The whole town lives in one big building." But Wayne was already climbing down from the rig.

Lonnie got out, too. In the parking lot, the fresh breeze exhilarated her. Mint-scented hope sailed in on the wind. She turned so it cooled her face, turned again so it ruffled her hair. She'd stand right here in this strange, energized air flow forever, if she could. Upwards, puffy blackness rolled toward them, a celestial tsunami. The voice returned: *Here in big sky country, when you look down or all around you, you won't see much. You'll have missed the main attraction completely. You've got to look up.*

She felt it strongly now, this strange, excited anticipation. On an impulse, she said, "Now that you mention it, I think I'll stay here a while, too. Edmonton might be too much for me." She meant it jokingly, facetiously, as if Edmonton was a mere cowpoke town to her. She was from the suburbs of Denver but thought of herself as belonging somewhere far more urbane and hip. New York City or Los Angeles.

Wayne didn't get the joke. He didn't seem surprised that she wanted to stay in Nomads Nest, either. He said, "Let me buy you a good-bye snack then, neighbor. You'll be wanting to try the ketchup potato chips. Never seen 'em south of the border."

Wayne was a nice old man. He didn't try anything on her the whole twelve plus hours they rode together. Of course, it would have been especially icky if he had, since he kept saying she reminded him of his granddaughter. His granddaughter, who somebody un-ironically named Fleura-Dania, was into fiction writing. Lonnie had taken a couple of stabs at writing movie scripts herself, though her first love was acting. She'd only had bit parts in high school plays though and later, community theatre. Fleura-Dania attended a university in Calgary, pursuing a degree in Creative Writing instead of having to work like Lonnie always had, the lucky duck. Pampered princess was more like it, Lonnie thought, trudging after Wayne with the heavy canvas tote bag that carried the remains of her life. *Rocky Mountain High* was scrawled across the bag's side in loopy black letters, above a silhouette of a bear and a pine tree.

Wayne filled up his rig and Lonnie went to the ladies' room to freshen up after the long ride. She washed her hair in the sink. The pink liquid hand soap from the wall dispenser left her hair gummy, so she combed it straight back, as if she'd gelled it that way on purpose. She went on to take a whole whore bath with wet paper towels, snickering at the term "whore bath," then admonishing herself for being immature. She brushed her teeth and changed into clean jeans and a t-shirt. When she came out, it dawned on her that she didn't know why she was looking around for the old guy, when she'd decided to stay here. Oh right, he'd wanted to gift her some good-bye potato chips.

She found him talking to a thirty-ish Native guy who was behind the counter. Apparently, someone had set up a makeshift café and sleeping area downstairs, a storm party that folks around here were all excited about.

The Native guy got busy pulling cigarette packs out of cartons and sorting them into the little compartments on the wall behind him. "Let me treat you to a good-bye lunch, then," Wayne said to her.

"Wow. Thanks." They were down the basement steps before she remembered that he'd wanted to beat the storm to Edmonton. Then she remembered not to stupidly do herself out of a free lunch. She said, "Should you try to get yours to go?"

"Ah, yes. I'll ask about that."

The café looked like a regular basement and smelled like one too, vaguely musty. Half of the eight folding tables were occupied. A woman Lonnie's ex-mother's age handed them menus printed on half sheets of computer paper. The waitress sported the bedhead look, a trend Lonnie had forgotten about. Her ex-mother wore it for a while when Lonnie was in elementary school. She couldn't tell if the waitress looked a mess because she was hungover, like Lonnie's ex-mother would have been this early if it wasn't a workday. Or perhaps the woman just didn't know that deliberately mussed hair went out of style years ago. There were two lunch options, a chicken patty sandwich or a donair sandwich.

Wayne made her order the donair because she told him earlier that she'd never had Canadian food. She didn't even know there was such a thing as Canadian food. Well, he really just suggested the donair sandwich but it seemed rude to reject his enthusiastic suggestion when he was paying.

Donair was some kind of meat mixed with some other stuff. She'd rather have chicken than mystery meat, so she tried to drop a hint, hoping he'd say, "Ha-ha, geez, seems like maybe you should get the chicken after all." She said, "Oh, a meat mix. Like your dog food!" Wayne was hauling tons of packaged dry dog food.

She was only kidding but he looked sad. She felt bad for hurting his feelings. To make up for it, she acted all eager to try the Canadian icewine he'd recommended. The only other drink choice was Coke, which she'd also rather have. It was better not to get fuzzy headed in strange surroundings. Oh well, she'd just take a sip or two.

He ordered for them both. The ratty-haired waitress pointed her ballpoint pen at Lonnie and said, "Poo teen?"

Like Lonnie really needed this witch's weird insults right now. She said, "Excuse me?"

"Poo teen?"

To think she'd come all this way, only to run into a doppelganger of the evil ex-mother she left behind in Denver. "Excuse me but I'm not any kind of teen. I'm twenty-five years old, poo old woman." She dug furiously through her tote bag, searching for her drivers' license, her face burning.

"Yep, we'll both have it! Thanks, darlin'," Wayne said, overly cheerful, no doubt trying to smooth over the conflict. Lonnie remembered that Wayne lived in this building. She cringed. The woman was probably his neighbor. Oh, well. After all, neighbor or not, the waitress was the one who started it. The waitress, the *poo* waitress, continued standing there, staring Lonnie down until Wayne said, "Thanks, Karen! Oh, and would it be possible to wrap mine up to go? The lady will be eating here."

"The lady," the waitress muttered, stalking off.

He said, "You'll like poutine. It's the unofficial dish of Canada, you know. French fries covered with gravy and cheese curds."

"Oh. Well. Sorry."

"Well, that's okay."

Cheese curds. Eww.

They were quiet then, until he shook her hand and left.

She watched him go, through the high-up basement windows. Rather, she watched the lower half of a Wayne-shaped blur, legs moving fast in the downpour, bagged lunch swinging. The tables were full now and even more people sat on a raised, carpeted platform, a small stage. They looked small town poor. Orderly. Not trash poor. The men wore collared shirts. Several had creased hair, from where they'd removed their caps upon coming indoors. The women boasted a smattering of brightly colored costume jewelry. There was light chatter, a tinkling of laughter. Above it, she heard, "Mercy, how time flies, and "How's that new grandbaby?" If it wasn't for the portable plastic coolers filled with beer on ice she'd have taken it for a Baptist social hour in a church basement.

The donair and the poutine were okay, not great. But then she wasn't much of a foodie. She preferred to stick with tried and true food options. But the icewine, drinking one glass made her want another, enough to catch the dreaded waitress's attention. It reminded her of the cheap sweet wine she and her girlfriends would make the guys provide them with, back in her high school days. She wondered if teenage girls still demanded wine instead of beer to demonstrate that they were a cut above average, too classy to chug beer with the boys. Too dumb to realize cheap Kool-Aid wine wasn't classy.

Karen, the waitress, didn't speak to Lonnie when taking her money. But it didn't affect Lonnie's mood, which had taken a turn, catching the vibe of the wild weather outside. She flipped her gummy hair back and held her fork between her pointer and tall-man fingers, a pretend cigarette, since she'd misplaced her real ones and smoking probably wasn't allowed in here anyway. She was a Hollywood dame in an old black and white movie. The voice-over said, *The brunette beauty weeps in the ballroom as the clouds weep outdoors, in remembrance of her dear, departed father.* Then Lonnie teared up for real because Wayne did resemble her father, who died last year, the first step in the dismantling of her life. The resemblance wasn't in looks or mannerisms but something deeper. Basic goodness, decency.

It looked like nightfall through the high-up basement windows now, though it was barely one in the afternoon. A hard thunderclap shook the building. The lights went out.

The Native guy from upstairs came around with a tray of lit candles, anchored in jars that were half-filled with pebbles. When he set one on her table, their gazes locked above the flame.

Her mind reeled, a déjà vu from when she first met Stan. She felt herself falling for it again, even as she recognized that she was falling for it again, as if under a spell. It was too much to pull away from, the heady rush of a handsome man's intense interest.

He said, "Wayne said you can stay at his place. The key's under his doormat, apartment number one. My name's Oliver. Let me know if you need anything." His look lingered.

Then he moved on to the next table and she dropped her cigarette fork. It clattered to the floor, jarring her back to reality. As it turned out, Stan's intense gaze had been more like Stan staring straight through her, as if she was barely there at all. Wayne though, now he was an outstanding human being. It was nice to know there were still some of those around. She hadn't even thought about where she'd stay. Her mind was all over the place. But since that was sorted out now, she downed the rest of her second glass, then held up her empty glass for a third.

Karen brought another icewine in a fresh, chilled glass. Friendly now, she said, "That'll be a loonie and a toonie." She did a little dance along with her words. Lonnie smelled booze on the waitress's breath. It pissed her off. She handed over a US five dollar bill. Karen danced away with it, snapping her fingers, though there was no music.

The eerie wail of a tornado siren sounded. Oliver brought out a ladder and started hammering sheets of plywood over the insides of the windows. It seemed like the plywood should go on the outside of the building, not the inside, but what did she know.

Karen addressed the room. "Sleeping bags are on that back shelf, for those who didn't bring one. And we've got brown bag meals for two toonies: A nut butter and jam sandwich or a bologna and cheese sandwich, with an apple and chips. Otherwise, the kitchen's closed, except for drinks."

People mingled, joining others at their tables or chatting with whoever flopped down near them on the carpeted platform. They all seemed to know each other. There were about three dozen people here, triple the population of Nomads Nest, according to the sign on the highway. Karen brought out an old boombox, from which Air Supply grieved over lost love. With the candlelight and music, the place took on a subdued party atmosphere. Lonnie remembered thinking of her ex-mother as "the Abyssinian" when she'd worn the goofy bedhead hairstyle that Karen still sported. It was because of Beer Boy, the tan-colored Abyssinian guinea pig Lonnie had at the time. The Abyssinian guinea pig breed had cowlicks all over its fur, called "rosettes." They looked cute on Beer Boy, though.

A big girl with white-blonde hair plunked herself down in Wayne's vacated seat. "How's it hangin'?" boomed out of her cheery, doughy face. She was a plump sugar cookie girl, pulled from the oven too soon, practically a cartoon character.

"I really hope it's not hanging at all," Lonnie replied, in mock horror. She resisted the urge to push the girl's bellybutton to see if she'd giggle like the Pillsbury dough boy in the old commercials.

The girl lit a joint, took a hit on it and handed it to Lonnie. Lonnie was tipsy, so the audacity of the act thrilled her. She snatched the joint, took a deep toke, then passed it back. "Um, is this legal?"

"I don't give a shit." The girl beamed, seeming delighted with her reply.

Lonnie said, "What's your name?"

"Puddin' tane."

The expression of utter exhilaration returned. The girl seemed quite happy with her goofy joke.

"It's Shawna," the girl said. "What's yours?"

"Lonnie."

"Lonnie? Never heard that before. What's it short for?"

"Um, lawnmower?"

Shawna laughed, choking on the smoke she'd just inhaled.

"Hey, do you know that Karen woman?" Lonnie hoped the girl would say something nasty about her. The woman got on Lonnie's last nerve.

Shawna passed the joint back. "Yeah. She's a bitch."

Lonnie leaned forward, a bit giddy. "Oh, really?"

"Yeah. She's my mom."

Lonnie whooped, joined by Shawna.

Someone had put away half the tables, to clear the way for dancing. A couple of people got up and followed along with Oliver, who was demonstrating the dance

steps to a golden oldie, "The Loco-Motion." Shawna and
Lonnie joined the impromptu dance class but Lonnie
avoided eye contact with Oliver. The possibility of falling
for him was too much. She was still a wreck from the last
guy.

Lonnie was surprised to find out Shawna was only a
year younger than her. Shawna took her back to her high
school days. Since then, Lonnie's younger brothers and
sister were the ones having this kind of fun, while Lonnie
played the role of second mother. She and Shawna drank,
smoked and danced by candlelight, along with some
others, including a skinny octogenarian male who only
seemed to know the funky chicken dance.   Lonnie
couldn't remember the last time she'd had such a blast. It
reminded her of the teenage parties she'd gone to, when
somebody's parents weren't home, though most of the
people here were older adults.

Later, Shawna procured a flashlight, and they went
upstairs to the convenience store. She followed Shawna's
lead in snitching a six-pack of beer, a pack of smokes and
two Hostess cherry pies. They hung out at Shawna's
parents' dark apartment for a while, then went back to the
basement and snitched a couple of the brown bag meals.

Bowls of peanuts in the shell had appeared on the
tables. Lonnie joined Shawna in throwing peanuts at
people when they weren't looking, then howling at their
reactions when they tried to figure out what had just
bounced off their heads. Lonnie decided everyone should
be sixteen again, once in a while.

Later still, the music was off and everyone had settled
into sleeping bags for what was left of the night. Shawna

snuck off with Oliver. They kissed, up against the wall, then disappeared together. Lonnie had learned by then that Oliver was married, with a new baby. She wondered if his wife and child were alone upstairs, with the power out.

It hit her like a slap then, how much Shawna was like her ex-friend and co-worker, She Whose Name Shall Not Be Spoken. The similarities didn't show at first. The Unspeakable one was very polished. She took her fashion seriously and worked as an executive administrative assistant, like Lonnie had. Shawna wore an army-green men's t-shirt and did odd jobs for a living, like picking up dog doo-doo. She'd had Lonnie rolling with laughter about it earlier. The traits Unspeakable and Shawna shared were more at the core. That naughty but innocent attitude that drew you to them, like they were just a barrel of devilish fun but harmless, at the same time. That type wasn't harmless at all, though. In their carefree, careless way, they'd destroy your life.

Shawna returned after a while and slipped back into her sleeping bag. Lonnie's disgust faded, as sleep crept up on her. Then, all she heard was soft breathing all around her. She felt overwhelmed with gratitude, safe and cozy due to the kindness of strangers, while a storm raged outside.

A vision of her life popped up in her mind, on a map, like the maps she'd brought up on her phone, on her ride with Wayne. Before this, her life had been on a straight side road with mostly small dots, small events, like the small towns on the maps.

But it led up to a large dot, comparable to a large city, though not a good one. It was a big tangled knot, intolerable, so she bolted. This time, she moved along physically too, hitching a ride in an eighteen-wheeler.

She found herself on a side road again now. Calmed at finding a way to visualize the chaotic state of her existence, she drifted off to sleep.

In the morning, she woke to Shawna's dough face, close up, small blue eyes gleaming. She knew Shawna's type now, dangerous underneath. But Shawna's overly exuberant expression made Lonnie laugh in spite of herself.

Shawna handed her a cup of coffee in a mug with a yellow smiley face on it. Before Lonnie could thank her, Shawna practically shouted, "Let's be roomies! There's an apartment upstairs we can have, apartment number six. And we can have it. Right. Now." She poked Lonnie's chest twice, with those last two words.

Lonnie wasn't awake enough to answer such a complicated proposal. She was just trying to sit up without spilling coffee all over the sleeping bag. A few other people were still there, gathering up their things and saying their good-byes.

Shawna said, "My dad said we can have it for only $750 a month. He said that's even less in US dollars, $500, split two ways. Practically free! Yeah?"

Shawna's parents were probably just dying to unload her. "Hold on," Lonnie said. She took her coffee with her to the bathroom. She needed a minute to think.

She only had a couple thousand dollars to her name. Wayne had surely only meant to offer her a place to stay for a night or two, no more than that. She had to do something, and quick. Her reflection in the mirror startled her, like she was so out of context that she didn't recognize herself. She should be at the Best West Insurance Company headquarters in downtown Denver right now, in her crisp navy Tuesday skirt and matching heels. She should be having her morning coffee at her computer, forcing herself to focus on the list of work-related phone calls in front of her. Pushing her real life out of her mind until lunch time. Then she'd be able to answer the question from the florist and deal with the cousin who was upset about kids not being invited to Lonnie's wedding.

She remembered her mental road map from the night before, and her current position on it, splashed her face with water, rinsed her mouth. *And this is where our heroine's real story begins*, said the voice-over narrator in her mind.

"Yeah!" she said to Shawna on her return, poking Shawna's chest with her forefinger. Picturing herself doing it as she did it, back in the starring role.

Shawna squealed, bouncing up and down on the sleeping bag. The voice-over said, *And this, my friends, will have to do for now.*

Back From the Dead

TJ was lying in bed with baby Tony, who she'd just finished nursing. "Who's Mama's good boy? Who's Mama's Tony-pony-macaroni?" she cooed. He gazed at her in that super serious way of his, so comical on a seven-week-old baby. Then his face broke into a big, toothless, open-mouthed smile. His first smile. To TJ, it was like sunshine bursting through storm clouds.

It reminded her that there was something good in her life. Something amazing. Her phone rang but she ignored it. Whoever it was could just frigging wait because her baby was smiling at his mother for the very first time. She was still stunned that she was somebody's mother now. She loved him so much it hurt.

Immediately after her phone stopped ringing, Oliver's phone rang in the other room. So that would be goddamn Greta from upstairs. When Greta wanted to talk to you, Greta expected to talk to you.

Oliver came in and handed her his phone. "It's goddamn Greta," he said, trying to joke with her. She planned to stay here in the bedroom, away from Oliver, until he went to work.

"What," TJ said into the phone.

"TJ! I just tried to call you, girl. Listen, Max and I want to go to town. Can you watch Emma?"

"Town" was Calgary, over an hour away. So they'd be gone at least a few hours. The money she'd earn would be a nice little addition to TJ's secret stash. Every dollar counted, or every loonie, as they said here.

"When?"

"Whenever you can get here. We're ready to go."

"I can be there in about twenty minutes."

"Perfect. Thanks, sweetie."

She handed the baby to Oliver so she could take a quick shower. Oliver was acting super humble and caring, after not coming home until dawn again, though his shift ended at midnight. "Acting" humble and caring was accurate. If he really cared, he'd have come home after work. He held his son stiffly, awkwardly. He wasn't used to holding his son. He didn't really know how.

#

Emma was three and fascinated with baby Tony. When TJ nursed him, Emma pulled up her top and "nursed" her doll.

Greta and Max didn't get home until seven p.m., which was nine hours of babysitting, $45 in US dollars. TJ still thought in US dollars, after nearly a year here. Greta and Max brought home a scraggly black kitten they'd found wandering around in a Tim Hortons parking lot. Emma was beside herself with excitement, chasing after it and shrieking "Baby cat! Cat baby!"

TJ snatched Tony up from his folded-up blanket on the floor, before he contracted some kind of horrible disease from the mangy feline. She strapped him into his baby carrier. Then she just stood around, waiting for Greta to pay her.

Greta snapped at Max, "Just give it a rest. Jiminy Christmas." Max's staring into the breast pocket of his shirt had brought on Greta's outburst. TJ had seen this strange exchange between the two of them before. What was he checking for in there? Another woman's phone number? A packet of cocaine?

Greta finally seemed to notice that TJ was waiting. Greta made a fake-cheery face. "Thanks so much, sweetie. You saved the day for me. Now, where did I put my purse…"

Greta handed TJ a roll of bills. TJ opened the door, her tacklebox full of jewelry-making supplies in one hand, Tony in his carrier in the other. She headed downstairs. She hadn't gotten around to working on her jewelry. Emma and Tony napped at different times. She also cleaned the place, hoping for a nice tip. There wasn't that much cleaning to be done, but Greta did give her a few extra loonies. After Tony was asleep, TJ would put on some tunes and make jewelry at the kitchen table. There was some tiger tail ice cream still in the freezer too, if Oliver hadn't already slurped it down his snout.

An older man stood outside her apartment. At first, she thought it might be Jack, who, along with his wife Karen, owned the whole place.

It wasn't Jack though. The man held a suitcase. The scenario just didn't look right. TJ started back up the stairs, back to Greta's.

The man saw her. "TJ," he called. He knew her name. Her heart lurched. The tacklebox fell out of her grasp and clattered down a couple of steps. She nearly dropped the baby, too. The man was her father but he couldn't be her father. Her father was dead.

She was afraid to go closer but she couldn't bear to walk away, either. Tony started fussing.

The man said, "What's dis here, huh? My Tori Janelle, my Tanya Jade, all grown up. And who ya got witcha dere… is dat my grandson?"

Tori Janelle and Tanya Jade were names TJ had called herself at different times in her childhood. Her parents could never agree on anything, not even on what to name her. They finally just gave her initials. Fine then, they'd simply let her pick out her own name, they said. None of the names she picked for herself stuck, though. To her, her real name had always just been TJ.

She put Tony up on her shoulder and patted his back, stalling. TJ didn't know how to react to the unreality in front of her. Her dad had died when she was fifteen, five years ago now. He stepped closer. She held up her hand, signaling him to stop. She'd seen enough zombie movies to know that you didn't want to let them get too close. Which was ridiculous. This was ridiculous.

He stepped back. "Okay kid, I'll level witcha." She'd almost forgotten his tough guy way of talking, his "disses," "dats" and "witchas." He was from New Jersey, originally.

He said, "I, uh, I got in some trouble. Hadda leave town. I didn't wanna leave ya, kid. I *had* to, unnerstand? It broke my heart. But I'm back, see. I'm gonna make it up to ya."

"We thought you died. We had a memorial service."

"Yeah."

Yeah. That's all he had to say? *Yeah?* "How did you find me?"

"Your mudda. She said you married an Eskimo or sometin' and moved up here to the nort pole widdem." She'd almost forgotten about his lopsided smile too, how he only smiled with one side of his mouth. It made him look like he was being sarcastic, but it was just how his face operated.

His kidding around reminded her of the good old days, Before. Her life used to be divided into Before Dad Died and After Dad Died. Now it was divided into Before Tony Was Born and After Tony Was Born. She just realized that. Her mind ping-ponged between the present to the past and back again. She said, "This could definitely be the north pole, in the wintertime. Which is about nine months of the year." As if that mattered at all right now.

Strange that her mom had told her dad where to find her but hadn't mentioned him to her. She'd just talked to her mom on the phone a couple of days earlier. "Are you and Mom back together?"

He laughed. It wasn't a happy laugh. "Ah. Dat would be a no."

Her mom had had a live-in boyfriend for a couple of years, but of course Dad hadn't been an option then. Her mom and dad used to fight constantly. Her mom and

Bruce never fought. "Oh. Well, are you in any danger? From any outlaws or… anyone?"

"Nah. Dat's all over and done wit, most likely. Say, how 'bout letting your old man in, huh? I come a long way to see ya."

She unlocked the door and gestured him into the apartment, hoping it wasn't too messy. She said, "Oh, and to answer your question, yes, this is your grandson. Anthony Vincent Falcon."

"You named him after me?"

His tough guy eyes teared up and she struggled not to fall apart.

#

TJ and Oliver only had the one bedroom, so her dad slept on the couch. He'd been there for three weeks. The longer he was around, the less Oliver was around. Not that Oliver was around that much anyway. Oliver had come stumbling in at five that morning, when TJ was awake, nursing Tony in their bedroom. She didn't say anything. She wouldn't engage in vigorous screaming matches the way her parents had. She didn't have the energy for it.

Anyway, she got it. Oliver didn't want her anymore. Screaming wouldn't change it.

They'd met when Oliver was staying with her neighbors in Tucson, where TJ lived with her mom and, later, Bruce. The neighbors were Oliver's cousin and the cousin's wife, Eli and Rose. She and Oliver had only gone out a few times, so she was shocked and horrified to find herself pregnant.

But Oliver said he was thrilled. He'd practically begged her to marry him and move back here to Canada with him, where he could legally work. He was twelve years older than her, so she never dreamed that he wouldn't know what he was asking for. But she guessed he didn't know, because he'd soon seemed to change his mind about wanting a wife and baby. Or maybe it was her, specifically, that he changed his mind about.

TJ and her dad were watching TV and making jewelry, as they did for several hours per day now. Her online shop was starting to turn a profit, with her dad's help. He wanted her to upgrade to sterling silver and semi-precious beads, and move on to real gold findings, after that. That way, she'd make more money on each item. He suggested she keep the costume line too, at least for a while. She couldn't afford to upgrade, though. Not yet.

Her dad looked up from a name necklace, a special order. He was tying knots in the thin black cord, between letter beads, S-L-O-A-N. They were debating whether it was a cool name (her) or a stupid name (him). She said it was original without being cutesy. He said it was a name for a bank teller with loose morals. As if it was related to the discussion, he said, "Speaking of crap, dat guy you're married to, he's a bum."

"Dad, can we not do this again? I'm stuck here, for now at least. You know that, right?"

"No, I don't know dat. Because I ran into Jack and Karen downstairs at the store. And Jack and Karen told me that the old couple upstairs moved out, apartment number four. Climbing two flights of steps had got to be too much for 'em. And, it just happens to be a two-bedroom unit." He pulled a key out of his pocket and dangled it in the air, triumphant.

It took a minute for his meaning to sink into TJ's mind. She said, "Yeah, I saw the moving truck. But what? I mean, how? I didn't think you had any money."

"Who toldja dat? I got plenty money. I just ain't giving none of it to that guy you married. He's a bum."

TJ had been stashing money, on her mom's advice, in case Oliver left her. But she hadn't even considered leaving Oliver. She couldn't legally work in Canada yet, so she hadn't had a choice. But now, suddenly, she did. It was too much to take in all at once. She said, "I don't know."

Her dad gave her a long look. He said, "Well, you tink about it."

#

TJ helped her dad furnish his apartment. Or, more accurately, her dad helped her furnish his apartment. He drove her around in his car and tended to Tony in the stores, while she shopped. They shopped nearly every day for two weeks. They bought a dinette set, a living room set, two bedroom sets and a TV. They bought bedding, lamps, wall art, towels and dishes.

Everywhere they went, she'd start by asking him questions about the specifics. And he'd answer, "I don't know, kid. Whatever you want."

They didn't go to the top-of-the-line stores but they didn't scrounge at resale shops either, like she and Oliver had had to do. It was very satisfying to furnish a whole place at once, with all new stuff. Picking out what she liked without much attention to price tags seemed like make-believe, after a year of barely scraping by with Oliver. She felt like a child who was playing house.

She decorated her dad's place in mostly grey and navy blue. Grey was the main neutral color in the stores right then, so it was easy to match. She picked navy to go with it because it seemed a no-nonsense color, appropriate for a mature man's home. Then she read online that the rule for interior design colors was: 60/30/10. So, sixty percent grey and thirty percent navy. For the other ten percent, she decided on red. That should give it some inviting bright pops of color, according to the internet.

Now it was done and she couldn't stop wandering around, admiring it. She didn't like to brag so she didn't say it out loud, but it was so coordinated and nice that it reminded her of something you'd see in a model home. She even thought that maybe she'd found her calling. Maybe at some point, when Tony was a little older, she'd see about becoming a professional interior designer.

Her dad didn't bring up her moving in with him again. But he said he wanted a twin bed for the spare bedroom, one of few things he'd weigh in on at all. It went through her mind that if a larger bed was in that small bedroom, there wouldn't be space for a crib. She wondered if he was doing all this for a reason, letting her pick out everything for the new place so she'd feel like it was her place, too. If so, it was kind of working.

#

Her final break-up with Oliver just sort of happened. She was upstairs at her dad's with baby Tony over half the time anyway, by then. Oliver was hardly ever home and her dad's apartment was a lot more comfortable than hers was. He took her grocery shopping, too. Oliver's car had broken down before the baby was born and there had never been enough extra money to get it fixed. There was a public bus stop nearby, but taking the bus was a real pain with a baby, and nearly impossible with a baby and groceries.

Her dad adamantly refused to buy anything for "the bum" though, and she was too proud to beg. So she'd buy cheap groceries for herself and Oliver, out of Oliver's small paychecks. And her dad filled his cart with groceries for his apartment. Her dad could afford better food than she could. And he made homemade pizza, fried shrimp and beef stroganoff. The man could cook, something she didn't remember about him from Before. He'd also bought a washer and dryer.

She slept over at her dad's most nights, her and baby Tony. She'd never liked being home alone, though she didn't tell anybody because it sounded childish. It was an irresistible luxury to be in such cushy surroundings, and even more of a luxury to not be afraid. The main draw was her dad himself, though. Having him back after thinking he was dead was unbelievable great luck, truly a dream come true. Even though he'd lied.

There was a better view here, too; he was up a story higher. Another storm was rolling in. Her dad was on the sofa with baby Tony and she was on the loveseat, painting her fingernails a bright fuchsia color, pleased to own the fancy nail polish her dad had paid for. The TV was on but they were more interested in the sky show on the other side of the big picture window. Her dad said, "Look at dat. It looks like dat cloud's caught in dat damn maple tree."

The cloud did appear to be twisted around the sugar maple's branches, as if it really did get itself good and trapped there.

While admiring that oddity, a black streak caught her eye. It was a black squirrel. "Dad, look," she said. She'd tried to point out the black squirrels to him before but they'd gotten away before he got around to looking.

"Ah, yeah. I see him now."

The squirrel scampered toward the maple tree, climbed up its trunk, then was lost in the tangled tree cloud. At first, Nomads Nest seemed like it could easily win first prize for the dullest place on the planet. Nothing but flat, empty prairie for miles around, with only a thin grey strip of mountain showing in the distance. But then you started to see the details.

"Dad. You know I've gone downstairs a few times in the past couple days, right?"

"Yeah. So?"

"So, Oliver hasn't been home. Nothing's been touched. It's been three days. Two nights, for sure. Most of his clothes are gone. Do you think he's left for good?"

"He's a bum." Her dad turned back to watching the storm approach, as if he wasn't the slightest bit interested in her marital problems.

She took a deep breath. Her marriage to Oliver was just worn out. Why keep hobbling along with it, when she knew it was over and he obviously felt the same way. She said, "Could you maybe help me move Tony's crib up here?"

Her dad was off the couch and at the door instantly. He said, "I got it, kid. You stay here wit baby Tony. Oops, gotta get my screwdriver."

He carried the crib up in three trips and re-assembled it in the spare bedroom, whistling the whole time. That was something else she'd forgotten about, his whistling. She made a few trips downstairs herself then, carrying her clothes and the baby's things. She left everything else for Oliver. There wasn't much extra storage space in her dad's apartment. She didn't really feel like putting Oliver through extra hardship, anyway. She just wanted to move on. Getting married was a mistake that she and Oliver made. Going by his actions, he thought them having a baby was another mistake. But baby Tony wasn't a mistake to her. He hadn't been, since they first laid him in her arms.

#

A week later, she met with a divorce attorney. Her dad went out a couple of days after that to buy lobsters, to cook for dinner. He said it wasn't to celebrate her break-up with Oliver, but to celebrate her new beginning. She thought it was to celebrate her break-up with Oliver, though. Her dad couldn't stand him. She tried to put myself in her dad's shoes. She couldn't envision Tony having a baby with a spouse who didn't want either of them, since he was only a baby himself. But if someone hurt him, she'd fucking smash them.

Through the picture window, she watched her dad's car exit the parking lot. It was grey outside, getting ready to rain. She called her mom. Her mom hadn't returned TJ's calls since TJ's dad had appeared, about two and a half months now. Before that, they'd talked every couple of weeks. There was some kind of weirdness going on.

Her mom answered now and acted like nothing was off at all. As they went through the usual small talk phase of their conversation, TJ peeked in on Tony, who was napping in his crib. She put a mug of hot water in the microwave, then picked through the fancy basket of assorted tea bags. Her mom was doing okay. Her mom's boyfriend was doing okay. Her mom's poodle, Oodle, was doing okay.

When TJ couldn't take any more small talk, she cut in. "Mom. Dad's here and baby Tony and I have moved in with him. Why didn't you tell me he came back from the dead?"

There was a long silence. Then her mom said, "When he asked me for your address, I thought he wanted to send you a card or something. I had no idea he'd move up there!"

"Okay. But why didn't you give me a heads-up ahead of time, even if you did think it was just going to be a card? You and I talked after he contacted you."

"Oh, TJ, I don't know. His coming back brought up issues that had already been put to rest."

"Did you know he wasn't dead?"

"Let's not get into all that. It's ancient history."

She knew. Then TJ thought of something else. The spending spree after her dad's supposed death. Even as a fifteen-year-old, she knew they weren't the kind of people who made flashy, high-end purchases, let alone a few of them one right after the other. They were the kind of people who felt lucky to finally be able to own a modest, older, two bedroom house. But there was the new Lexus, the sunroom built onto the house, her mom's "mourning ring," which was a Tahitian pearl surrounded by diamonds. If her mom knew her dad wasn't dead, then that would be... *insurance fraud*. A felony. It somehow didn't surprise TJ that her dad most likely got himself involved in something shady, not really. But her *mom?*

It overloaded her brain. It was too much, on top of her dad's re-emergence from the dead and now, the break-up of her marriage. She shut it off. She visualized a wall switch in her mind and flipped it to "off."

"Are you there?" her mom said.

"Barely," she said. She took a deep breath, and changed the topic. She started telling her mom about her impending divorce.

Her mom listened through two cups of hot tea. The jasmine tea, then the cinnamon orange.

When TJ was talked out, her mom said, "Oh, I know how it is. Your father was the same way."

"He was a great father, at least, though. Remember all the horsey rides I took on his back, and him carrying me upside down through the house, and tickling me until I couldn't breathe?"

TJ heard one of her mother's long-suffering sighs. She'd never really yelled. At TJ, that is. She just did those pained, drawn out sighs. She said, "There's more to parenting than being a fun playmate."

"Oh. Wow. You have a point there. And I know he...left and that was really hard. But he's really trying now. I mean, I was super miserable and trapped and he frigging *saved* me. He really did."

"Listen, I've got to run. But you kiss that precious baby for me!"

The call ended abruptly, leaving her scattered. They had just talked for quite a while, so she guessed her feelings shouldn't be hurt. But did her mom end the call just because she'd said something good about her dad?

She realized that she hadn't even thought to ask her mom for help, even though she'd always lived with her until she married Oliver. Whenever she'd talk about her problems with Oliver or anything else, her mom's advice was about what she could do for herself, not offers to help her. It was like her mom felt like her job was over when TJ moved out, and that was that. It really stood out, now that her dad had done so much for her. Now, that did hurt her feelings.

There was a knock at the door.

She peered through the peephole and there was Oliver, with his "I'm sorry" face on. She thought about not answering the door, but then she did. He said, "I saw that your dad was out. Are you doing okay?"

Oliver seemed like a stranger, this guy she married and whose child she'd carried. She wanted to say, *Who the hell are you, anyway?* She said, "I'm all right. Are you doing okay?"

"I'm okay. I got served with divorce papers."

"Hmm. That was fast." She shrugged, stepping aside to let him in.

He said, "Whoa. This place is nice."

She puffed with pride, then caught herself. "Do you want to see Tony? It's about time for him to get up."

"Nah, don't wake him. I might take him for a while this weekend, maybe. Or one day next week, if I have time."

"Sure," she said, though his words filled her with terror. Oliver, who didn't even know how to hold Tony, taking him off alone. Oliver and random women, taking her baby off for weekends, out of her sight. She began blabbing on, her voice high pitched. Soon she'd sound one of those clowns who swallowed helium, then talked funny at kid's parties. She squeaked, "If you don't have time, I understand. I mean, you might not be ready for fatherhood for ten more years. My dad wasn't. And that's okay!"

He stood there, nodding. He reminded her of a cardboard cut-out, or a bobble-head. It wouldn't be surprising, she thought, if baby Tony went looking for him in twenty years and found him still right here, in the same cheap apartment, at the same minimum wage job, wanting nothing more than to go drink beer after work. She popped her eyes at Oliver, expecting him to say something back like "Derp?" It cracked her up, and then she couldn't stop laughing.

Oliver looked confused now, possibly frightened. An easily befuddled dumbo! What had she ever seen in him? Had she ever seen anything in him? She felt like she'd aged a decade in the past year. Trusting Oliver, marrying him, having his baby, all that had taught her a few harsh lessons. But now that she had her son, she wouldn't turn those hands of time back, even if she could.

Through the picture window, they both watched her dad's car turn into the parking lot. The rain was pouring down outside now. Oliver said he thought he'd better go and he hurried away.

Blue O'Clock

Wayne's granddaughter, Fleura-Dania, got her artsy streak from him, he was pretty sure about that. Only her thing was writing fiction, whereas his was art. He'd strongly advised her to major in something practical, though. He'd majored in art years earlier himself, then had to turn to long haul trucking to make a living. He couldn't complain too much overall but being on the road so much got lonely. He also knew that being away from home so much had a lot to do with his marriage to Fleura-Dania's grandmother not working out.

Even after getting into some decent galleries, he'd never been able to make a living with his art, not even close. But he did it anyway, simply because he loved it. As he liked to tell people, he hadn't been paid for doing any of the things that meant the most to him. Only the lucky few were able to combine making a living with engaging in their life's passion.

With his latest art phase, working with colored waters, the few people he'd mentioned it to thought he meant he was painting with watercolors. But no, he meant colored waters. He had an exhibit at the upcoming Art Night, tonight in Calgary. They were held four times per year. People came from miles around to stroll from gallery to gallery, checking out the exhibits in a party-like atmosphere, with free wine and cheese. Sometimes a big shot art critic or dealer would come around, or even a movie star. You never know who might show up.

What a surprise it was for him this time, to see Fleura-Dania's name on the list of artists! She was scheduled to do some kind of reading. One didn't think of an Art Night as a writers' venue, but there it was, Fleura-Dania Wilcox, her name and picture on the flyer in front of him. Her reading would be at the Prince Albert Gallery at 8:00 p.m. He knew why she hadn't said anything to him. She was on the outs with her mother again. If it ever got out that she'd invited Wayne but not Sarah, oh-ho-ho, it'd be World War III between those two again. He planned to step away from his own exhibit for a while and surprise her anyway.

On the way out of the apartment building, he ran into the new guy in number four, Tony. The guy had that baby with him, as usual. It reminded Wayne of himself with Fleura-Dania, when she was just a tiny tot. Same situation too, his daughter had had to move in with him way back then, after breaking up with her loser husband. Tony said, "Hey dere, Wayne. Whatchu all spiffed up for?"

Wayne straightened his tie. He didn't wear his suit often and felt not quite himself in it. "I'm headed to the

Art Night in Calgary. Want to ride with me?" Wayne's pieces were set up at the Red Wheat Gallery. He'd get a kick out of watching Tony figure out that they were his. Wayne didn't talk about his art much to non-artsy people, though. They said too many clueless things, like "Where do you get your ideas?" Or "You should" followed by something stupid, like become a tattoo artist, paint a portrait of the advice-giver's dog or copy the style of Dali, Picasso or Georgia O'Keeffe, because "they got real famous, you know." Better to not even start that conversation.

"Ah, you're going to dat thing too, huh? I can't go, I got little Tony tonight. All the gals in the building went together, you know."

"They did? Geez, that's… five of them now, isn't it?"

"Yeah. My TJ, the owner's wife and the two gals in number six. And the one who has the little girl. They just left."

"Well, good. There's not enough for them to do for fun around here. Heck, we men should all go out for a beer sometime. There's us two and Jack, plus the two young ones, Oliver and Max in number five."

Tony said, "Hey now. I'll go if Oliver don't go."

"Oh geez. Sorry, I forgot."

"Eh, dat's okay. Just don't invite him, huh? He's a bum."

"You got it, Tony. See ya later." Wayne stopped to watch the Arctic hares, hopping around on the grass beyond the parking lot. You knew winter was finally over for good when their fur changed color. It was halfway changed now, the winter white mottled with brown, though it seemed late in the season for the change. The group of hares hung around because Karen fed them. She had them so spoiled they'd practically hop right up to you, expecting a treat. He'd looked it up once and learned that a group of hares was called a husk or a drove.

He cranked the music up on the drive, the Stones, Billy Joel, popular oldies. Art Nights brought up a mix of nerves and hope still, after all these years. He rarely had anything to be nervous about anymore, so that frame of mind made him feel young.

When he arrived, there was already a decent crowd. His exhibit, *Color Wheel on the Rocks*, was set up near the snack table. He filled a plastic cup with cheap wine and piled some cheese cubes and crackers onto a small paper plate. He'd forgotten to eat supper. An elderly lady with expensive looking jewelry spoke to the young guy who was with her. She said, "Look how the colors change as you walk around it. I've never seen anything quite like it!"

She was talking about one of his mobiles. Small, clear glass cubes were filled with water and food coloring, and lined up so that, for example, a blue cube and a yellow cube created the appearance of a green cube from one side, where you'd be looking through both the blue cube and the yellow cube at once. From a different angle, the yellow cube lined up with a red cube to make orange. It had four levels, with several clear cubes filled with different colors of water on each level. The mobile was held together with thin metal rods and clear fishing line.

The idea had come to him one night when he couldn't sleep. He'd had one of those sleep machines on at the time, the ones that projected moving, colored designs across the wall and ceiling. His daughter Sarah gave it to him for Christmas one year, thinking it might help his insomnia. The elderly lady said to the young man, "Oh, I adore that. How much is it?" A warm glow filled Wayne's chest. His art, and his girls, his daughter Sarah and granddaughter Fleura-Dania, they were what he lived for.

The young guy, most likely the lady's son or grandson, said, "$2,500! For that shit? Well okay, it *is* pretty, I'll give it that. But I'd call it… simplistic. It looks like it belongs in a daycare center."

The delight faded from the lady's face. She hobbled away. The young man stood there, watching the mobile and shaking his head.

Simplicity is a thing's essence, he wanted to plead. *It's deceptively simple; it's a direct soul-to-soul communication!* He clamped his teeth together to keep from snapping out a reply, which he knew was never a good look.

One artist had a meltdown at an Art Night a few years back, after someone mocked his bronze cowboy statues. It made the headlines, complete with a close-up photo of the artist's crazed face, eyes bulging, mouth wide open. The poor guy became the laughingstock of Calgary. He stopped exhibiting after that. Wayne understood, though. He'd worked on his current collection for months. Never mind the years and years he'd spent studying art and creating other collections. And then some young moron who no doubt bought his art at Walmart thinks he's qualified to casually dismiss it? For a delicious moment, Wayne visualized tapping the young bigmouth on the shoulder, saying, *How about if I knock your stupid bitch ass out, punk?* But of course, you had to play it cool, act like criticism didn't faze you at all. All but the greenest newbies knew that.

The gallery owner came over and started introducing Wayne around. For the next hour, he made small talk and shook hands, while internally slinking about, feeling like a cross between a beggar and a braggart. He disliked this part of the process. Creating art was when his spirit soared, free of the bullshit outer trappings. But trying to sell it was bullshit outer trappings. A couple of glasses of wine made it tolerable.

In a corner of the room, the lady who did the magnificent oil still lifes waved and he waved back. Her paintings were mostly of arrangements of kitchen items. She was so good that her paintings looked like photographs, and there was a subtly implied deeper, darker situation in each painting, too. He'd shelled out three grand, years ago, for one of Mari Albrecht's fruit and knife pictures. It hung on the wall above his kitchen table.

Next to her set up was the guy with the budget acrylic paintings. Wayne snickered to himself, picturing what the renowned Mari Albrecht must think about being placed next to a clod whose work looked like he'd painted it with his toes. The guy did trite local-ish scenes: A moose, a bear or a wolf under a full moon. Overly sentimental depictions of Native people, in full headdress or with a tear running down their cheek. Touristy junk. But boy, did it ever sell.

At ten 'til eight, he headed for the Prince Albert Gallery. It cost $25 at the door, which he didn't expect. He'd never seen a charge to enter a gallery on Art Nights, only jars for voluntary donations. This gallery's art pieces had been pushed to the sides to make room for rows of folding chairs, seating for four or five dozen people. Wayne took a seat in the back row. He knew how familiar faces could make one nervous, so he'd save his surprise show of support for afterwards.

The chairs filled up. The lights went off. A spotlight came on above the makeshift stage, where five wooden rocking chairs sat empty. A woman with glasses and a crisp, correct way of speaking picked up the microphone, a professor maybe, but she didn't introduce herself. Instead, she introduced *Basic Bitches*. That was the title of the anthology that would be read from. For another $25, you could get a paperback copy of *Basic Bitches* that was signed by the contributing authors.

The book's title rankled him. Fleura-Dania's name didn't belong with a low class book title. But he was eager to hear what his angel wrote, just the same. After having had a couple glasses of wine, he felt the need to share his pride. He nudged the woman next to him. "My granddaughter will be reading, Fleura-Dania Wilcox." She nodded but two other people shushed him. Geez. They didn't need to be so zealous about it.

The woman on stage said, "Without further ado," and the spotlight went off again, leaving the audience in darkness. When the light came back on, the five wooden chairs onstage held five women. Fleura-Dania was second from the left. Each woman held up an open copy of *Basic Bitches*. A collective gasp came from the audience. It took him a minute to catch on, because the women on stage had their hair and makeup done up all fancy, and had on dressy high heels, too. Well, that is, except for the mannish looking one with the buzz cut, in the middle chair. It took him a minute to catch on that none of the five women onstage were wearing a stitch of clothing.

His mouth went dry. He must be dreaming. Or possibly having a stroke.

The girl on the far left stood up. She sauntered up to the front center of the stage, taking her time as if she wanted to be sure no one missed out on seeing her stuff. She set her open book on the podium and began reading into the microphone. He wasn't interested in her story. He was interested in covering his granddaughter up with his suit jacket and dragging her off that damn stage.

"Sit down!" someone hissed. He did. He sat back down.

He noticed that the women on the stage seem to be seated youngest to oldest, from left to right. He wondered for a second if the stories were arranged that way too in the book, youngest to oldest authors or maybe youngest to oldest main characters. Then he remembered that wasn't important.

The naked high-heeled girl finished reading. Everyone seemed to be clapping wildly, except him. He was way over on the end farthest from the door, and the chairs were packed in tight. Leaving would create a disturbance. Fleura-Dania might notice.

Fleura-Dania got up and walked the short distance to the podium. Someone stage-whispered, "Look at the bird nest on that one." There was a flutter of shocked laughter, followed by a vigorous round of shushing. He felt a little better that someone else got shushed, too. He looked around to see which bottom-feeder he should throttle for talking nasty about his granddaughter. But he couldn't figure out who'd said it.

He closed his eyes. He didn't concentrate on her story. He didn't care about her story anymore. He'd just sit there and quietly die.

Finally, they reached the end of Fleura-Dania's shame. He was timing his escape. She turned and—shook her naked butt at the crowd.

The gallery erupted in boisterous applause. That's when he scurried out.

Back outside, he checked his phone. 8:20 pm. He had to get back to the Red Wheat Gallery soon. Artist attendance wasn't spelled out as a requirement. But there were many, many more artists who wanted a space in the galleries than there were spaces available. You'd want to mind your manners, if you hoped to be invited back.

He granted himself ten minutes to get it together. He made himself tune in on what was going on around him. The gallery next to the Red Wheat had some interesting wooden bowls with inlaid turquoise and copper. He considered getting one for Sarah. He decided against it, since it might lead to questions about where he'd gotten it. He didn't want to discuss this unfortunate evening. He went through applicable adages in his mind. You could only control yourself, and all that malarkey. He pulled himself together.

He was about to re-enter the Red Wheat when he heard his name called. It was the five gals from his building. They were loud and giggly, holding on to each other, weaving and wobbling down the sidewalk with wine-filled plastic cups. For a second, he was frightened. Then he laughed at himself. He must be getting old. Slipping back into his fake-ish outer persona, he called, "Good evening, ladies. I've gotta run but I'll catch you all back home. Enjoy!"

He heard some overly exuberant good-byes. Then Karen's daughter, Shawna, the pudgy one with the white-blonde hair, shouted after him:

Wayne, Wayne, water brain

Squeeze his head and watch it rain

Hyena-like laughter followed, from the whole dang bunch of them. Even that Lonnie girl, who he'd driven all the way up here from the states in the first place. Who he'd offered his apartment to, so she'd be safe after he'd continued on his route. Geez. He was just grateful the feral creatures weren't his granddaughters. Fleura-Dania's "exhibit" came back to him, a painful jolt. *Basic Bitches*. Was this just how things were now?

Well. He still had to get through another hour and a half at the gallery tonight.

He went back to the snack table near his exhibit and grabbed some more cheese cubes and crackers. And some more wine. A well-groomed fortyish couple discussed one of his pieces now. It consisted of long, clear glass rectangles full of colored waters. They were stacked horizontally in a clear frame on the wall. A small lightbulb with its own switch was located behind each long colored rectangle. As was explained in the framed placard, the light system was only temporary, to demonstrate how the colored rectangles worked. The rectangles were meant to be installed in front of a window, in the clear framework provided. The colored rectangles could be moved up and down within the frame, as desired. They were to be arranged so that a different colored rectangle lit up naturally each hour, as the sunlight hit them, as the sun made its daily journey across the sky.

The young man with the elderly lady would have probably said this one was simplistic or for a daycare center, too. But that was exactly the point. It was meant to recapture that childlike joy, upon seeing the magical yellow o'clock rectangle brighten at seven each morning. Or the blue o'clock lighting up at the eight p.m. cocktail hour.

The forty-ish woman said, "Honey! Could you just see that in the living room window? I don't know, I just feel happy when I look at it. You know?"

Her husband motioned to the gallery owner. "We'll take it," he said.

Wayne savored the shining moment, feeling for a moment like he'd been wrapped in a blanket of pure love. The feeling was one of a couple of things that he lived for.

Deep Cleaning

"It didn't look nearly this grungy with her furniture and stuff in here," Karen said, inspecting the stained bedroom carpet and grimy bathroom. She'd shut Shawna's bedroom door after Shawna moved out, and she'd left it shut for weeks. She preferred to get used to the proverbial empty nest gradually.

It actually helped that Shawna left her a mess to deal with. This way, she could be reminded of what a pain in the butt Shawna was and not miss her quite so much. It formed a neat seal over her deeper feelings, which were something akin to terror. She'd coasted along for twenty-four years, one year pretty much like the next. Then she was slammed with menopause and the empty nest at the same time. Those were two leaps closer to death, really, weren't they?

When Shawna came over to eat or borrow something, which she did nearly every day, Karen didn't tell her to clean up her old bedroom and bathroom.

"Make her clean it," said Jack, shaking his head. Jack was the Shay family's very own answer grape.

"Yeah, right. Make her do anything," Karen said.

"Want me to go get her?" Jack enjoyed the conceited delusion that he could control Shawna. And that Karen could control Shawna too, if only she'd follow his instructions.

Sometimes Karen told him how hard the empty nest was for her. Then he'd make his mock surprised face. He'd remind her how much she and Shawna had always butted heads. She found his reminders strangely comforting, too.

She said, "Yeah, right. You'll just drag her in here and make her clean. Sure you will. Remember when you tried to take her cigarettes away and she sprayed you down with the fire extinguisher? You were covered in that white chemical powder and coughing your head off. Hahaha."

"Fine then. Clean it all up yourself."

"Oh, don't worry. I'm sure I will."

Jack said, "Gotta say, I was kind of proud of her that time, though. She figured out how to use that fire extinguisher all by herself."

Karen especially loved him when he did that, kind of backtracked when she called him out on being a know-it-all. But then, he just had to say it. He said, "Covered in all that white powder, I looked like I could be her father."

She ignored him. Once in a while he'd make a remark like that and she never knew what he was after.

Reassurance that she and Shawna both definitely considered him Shawna's father? A show of perpetual gratitude? He'd known Karen was pregnant by someone else soon after he met her. Maybe he just felt like being a shithead.

He picked up his keys and went for the door, ready to start his daily rounds. He'd check the apartment hallways, the fuel pumps, the convenience store, the parking lot. The bald spot on the back of his head was a tempting target. She picked up the flyswatter and aimed it. He turned around. He pretended to be afraid, which made her laugh.

#

Deep cleaning Shawna's bedroom and bathroom took two days. Karen shampooed the carpet. She washed, ironed and re-hung the curtains. Only one boxful of leftover items was worth saving. On her way to put the box in the attic, she decided she'd clean out the attic, too. She hadn't been up this narrow stairway to the fourth half-story of the building in a decade.

It was Jack's idea to install Shawna into that apartment but Karen knew he was right. It was time. Roommate situations weren't known for their stability though, and neither was Shawna. But, they agreed, all they could do was try to get her to be as independent as possible. Either that or get a nice guy to marry her, which they'd be happy to do, if they met anyone suitable. Karen reasoned that if nothing else, at least Shawna's part of their apartment got a deep cleaning, before it started attracting vermin.

It was the same old attic. Dark, dusty and creepy, filled with the husks of past lives. Then again, she could always clear it out, paint it bright, give it a new purpose. She wondered for the first time if this empty nest thing might have a positive side to it. Entering a new stage of life did make you think about new possibilities.

Well, she'd clean the attic first, then see if the inspiration to remodel it stuck around. She set the box down and opened the windows. A good airing out, that was the first step. She stopped to admire the view of the Rocky Mountains from up here on the fourth floor. It wasn't much more than a grey stripe on the horizon from up here, either. But it was a mountain view, nonetheless.

The cool breeze flowed in. Invigorated, she returned to her apartment to gather her cleaning supplies. She passed by Shawna's apartment again, on the way back down. Shawna's roommate, that skinny Lonnie creature, opened their door, real abrupt, like she was mad and wanted to let Karen have it.

"Hello," Karen said, being polite anyway. The girl stood there in the doorway, hands on hips, glaring. It was the same silent hostility she'd treated Karen with, when they'd all gone to the Art Night in Calgary.

Karen had told Jack how strange and rude the girl was the first time she'd met her, when Lonnie called her a "poo waitress," after Karen asked if she wanted poutine with her sandwich. But Jack's difficult side came out then, too. First, he laughed like it was the funniest thing he'd ever heard. "Poo waitress, ha!" he brayed, nearly spitting his ravioli out on the kitchen table.

Then he pushed giving Lonnie a chance anyway, with the roommate situation. He said the girl had probably just had too much to drink. And he was right that there wasn't anybody else around for Shawna to be roommates with. Karen gave in, but if this attitude continued, she'd kick the girl out on her smart ass.

She walked on, getting back to her cleaning mission for the time being. She'd need Windex, paper towels, the broom and dust pan, trash bags. She hadn't had her morning coffee yet, so she microwaved some from the pot and poured it into a thermos. Loaded down with cleaning supplies and coffee, she trudged back up to the other floor of apartments. Fortunately, Loonie Lonnie kept her damn door shut this time.

From there, she proceeded up the narrow stairway to the attic again. She opened the attic door, regretting that she didn't think to bring her high-reach duster with its telescoping pole. She stepped in, set down her load and picked up the thermos, eager for that first sip of hot, sweet coffee with hazelnut creamer. The door slammed shut behind her.

She jolted, then relaxed. The wind coming in through the open windows had blown the door shut, obviously. That was all. That's what she was thinking, when something knocked her hard, on the forehead.

Then, she was on the floor in the fetal position, cradling her pounding head and trying to comprehend what the hell was happening. Someone yanked her arms behind her back. Karen thrashed and screamed, "Stop it! Stop!"

"Don't you even think about moving, poo old woman."

Karen exhaled. She said, "Oh. It's only you."

The girl shouted between deep breaths, like she was about to hyperventilate. She called Karen a "Karen", a drunk, a bitch.

Karen shook her arms free. She scrambled to her feet. At the same time, Lonnie pulled Karen's hair, calling her a "cauliflower head."

Karen shoved Lonnie, who lost her grip on Karen's hair. Karen said, "Good lord. Nobody's scared of you, you stretched out gum flapper. Grow up."

Lonnie bowed up, as if about to attack again but Karen was quicker this time. She stuck her foot behind Lonnie's foot, then shoved her again, this time making Lonnie fall on her bottom.

The thick thud Lonnie made upon landing, and the dumb look of shock on her face, struck Karen as hysterical. Karen laughed, and Lonnie began to cry.

Karen said, quite reasonably, she thought, "Well, you started it. That is what you get."

Karen felt her heartbeat slow back to normal, as Lonnie sat there on the floor, quietly sobbing into her hands.

Her feeling of safety restored, Karen's anger rose. How dare this creature, who was practically living off her and Jack's charity, mind, think she could glare at Karen, call her names, hit her...any of it!

Karen thought about kicking her in the face. She wouldn't even have to put much effort into it, since the girl was already sitting right there on the floor.

Alternatively, she might be able to strip her and make her walk back to her apartment naked. See how she liked that. But she couldn't muster up the energy for revenge. She didn't even know what they were fighting about. Also, Lonnie was about Shawna's age, just a kid to Karen.

Karen said, "You made me drop my coffee." She retrieved her thermos and sat on the floor too, sipping, waiting to hear what the kid's problem was. She was a bit intrigued now. And she had to admit, it was the most interesting thing that had happened to her in a while. Her head still hurt, though.

The girl lay down and stared straight up at the ceiling. Karen rolled her eyes. "That's a bit dramatic." It was a good thing Karen had experience dealing with a mildly disabled daughter. She knew that you should redirect inappropriate behavior instead of giving it too much notice. She said, "Get over there and start washing those windows."

The girl didn't move. Apparently, she had the audacity to feel sorry for herself, after everything she'd done. Karen lost patience. She said, "Move it, you… stink butt." She bounced the roll of paper towels off Lonnie's inert form, then picked up the broom and started brushing the walls down with it, top to bottom.

A conch shell lay on the floor, its outer lip broken apart from the rest of it. That must have been what Lonnie beaned her with. Karen didn't recognize it, a forgotten souvenir from some stranger's long ago tropical vacation. She envisioned a t-shirt, "Someone went to the Bahamas and all I got was knocked in the head with a conch shell." Actually, the Bahamas didn't sound half bad. Maybe she'd see about a vacation. After years of struggle, their finances had finally reached a level where Karen could seriously consider things like family trips to exotic locales.

#

After Lonnie finally got with it, she did a good job. A couple of hours later, the whole attic was dusted and swept. Karen and Lonnie talked now, companionably, sitting on the floor and sorting things into piles to be thrown away, donated or sold.

Karen told Lonnie she could take whatever furniture and housewares she wanted, under the condition that it all stayed in the apartment whenever Lonnie moved out. Karen wanted it for Shawna.

She said to Lonnie, "So, just to double check. We're friends now, right?"

"Right. And again, so sorry. Of course I know you're not my mother. To tell you the truth, I feel like I'm having some kind of drawn-out nervous breakdown. Not that it's an excuse or anything."

"What you've been through could drive anyone to a breakdown, hon. I get why you're upset about your fiancé, but if you don't mind me asking, why are you so angry with your mother?"

"Well, the last straw was when my fiancé cheated on me with my co-worker, who was also my good friend. We all worked together, at the Best West Insurance Company, maybe you've heard of it?"

"No, hon."

"Oh. Come to think of it, I think they're only in the states. Anyway, me, my fiancé, my co-worker/friend and my mother, we all worked there. What my mother did, first of all, was that she knew about the cheating for months but never told me, even when she knew I was planning my wedding."

"Well, that's rough. So your whole life kind of blew up on you at once, then? Let's see, your love life, your family life, your friendship, your job *and* your living situation? You lived with this guy right?"

"Yes, I did. And yeah, I lost everything at once, out of the blue. I also lost my younger brothers and sister, for now, at least. They're all still kids, so trying to contact them would kind of be dragging them into adult mess."

Karen was folding some of Shawna's baby clothes. Those were staying. She'd tried to put some of them into the "donate" pile but she couldn't do it. Funny how that worked, because she hadn't thought about them in years and probably wouldn't have even noticed if they were gone.

She said, "Now, with your mother, is it possible that her intentions were good? For example, could she have suspected but not been 100% sure? Like, maybe she was worried about possibly causing trouble over nothing?"

"I wish. But no. For one thing, when it all came out, she said I deserved it. She said I didn't make enough effort with my appearance. Just because I didn't always wake up early enough to do the whole nine yards with my hair and makeup. Then she said I didn't cook for him enough. She knew I worked longer hours than he did. She never liked me. It just took something that drastic for me to realize the extent of it. If that even makes sense."

"It does make sense, unfortunately. It does to me. I think some parents simply don't want the job. I can't imagine feeling that way myself, but my mother dumped me on my grandparents. My mother didn't even ask about me for years after that. It wasn't like she was a teenage mother or an addict or anything, either."

"Oh, I'm sorry."

"Thanks. I had a nice childhood anyway, though. My grandparents were great."

"My mother is different with the younger ones. She likes them."

"Ooh. I don't know if that's better or worse. Is she with their father?"

"No. We kids all had the same father. He died a little over a year ago."

"Hey, why don't you come over tonight? Shawna's coming. We can all fix dinner together. We could invite TJ and Greta too, if you want. I'll get Jack and Oliver to carry all this stuff down to your and Shawna's place."

"Thanks so much, Karen. I almost feel like I should start calling *you* Mom."

"Oh, hell no. Look what that little mix-up got me last time." Karen waved her off, embarrassed by the compliment.

Jack was home when Karen returned. He looked tired. She decided to apologize, before asking him to haul furniture around. She said, "I'm sorry about laughing at you hon, about the, er, fire extinguisher incident. It gets complicated, about Shawna. But you're right, I should have stayed on her about cleaning up her mess and, I'm sure, about a lot of other things too. Also, I'm thinking I might have been too quick to judge that Lonnie girl. She might actually be a good influence on Shawna. Fingers crossed, huh? Oh, I invited all the building's girls over to make dinner tonight."

He looked at her suspiciously. His eyes grew large. "What the hell! Just look at that goose egg on your forehead. I knew something was off. What happened, babe?" He stood up, like he was ready to go kick some ass.

She felt a surge of love for him, for that. It was easy to get caught up in the daily drudge, forget how fortunate you were, with who was in your life. He felt her and he had her back. Wasn't that what counted, in the end? She said, "Oh, nothing, hon. I banged into something in the attic. No biggie."

He checked her pupils, then made her lie in bed and watch TV while he brought her some pain meds and a nice glass of icewine. He fixed her a grilled cheese sandwich and a bowl of tomato soup, and brought it to her on a tray.

Her head didn't hurt now but she let him fuss over her a little bit more anyway. She set the alarm, so she'd be up when the girls arrived.

The Mothers' Circle

Greta didn't think TJ's jokey apology was cute. "Soory," TJ kept saying, sing-songy, buckling baby Tony into the backseat next to Emma.

TJ and Greta had joked about how people around here apologized constantly, in their Canadian accents. But Greta wasn't in the mood for jokes now, after waiting in the car for thirty minutes with a cranky three-year-old

Greta shouldn't have invited TJ again. TJ made them late last week too. Great first impression. She also hadn't given Greta any gas money, though Greta had asked her twice. Then again, the girl was barely out of her teens. She'd seemed a lot more mature before her father came up here and rescued her from Olive Brain.

Suddenly, a pale moon face appeared in Greta's driver's side window. An unusual squawk escaped Greta's mouth, from panicked shock.

Of course, TJ just had to mimic her. "Eep!" she said. "Eep! Soory!" This was why Greta was desperate for new friends. Hopefully, grown-up ones.

The face in the window belonged to Shawna. Greta started rolling down the window to see what Shawna wanted but Shawna had already opened the back door. It figured that TJ left it unlocked.

Shawna managed to wedge herself in on the floor of the car, even with the two little ones back there in their car seats. Greta said, "Um, may I help you?"

"I heard you were going to a mom's group. I want to come."

"But you aren't a mom, sweetie."

"I have to come! I'm pregnant."

Pregnant? Jiminy Christmas. Karen would flip her lid if that was true. Greta didn't think it was true, though. Shawna liked to try to get attention.

She cringed at the thought of showing up with a non-invited non-mother, and a crazy one at that, on top of being late again. But Shawna was prone to drama when she didn't get her way. Greta doubted Shawna would get out of the car. She decided to just go. She started driving.

TJ said, "Hey, did you guys ever notice that hardly anybody in our building is even Canadian?" No doubt she was trying to direct the conversation to something besides her wrongdoings, which Greta was about to bring up.

"I'm a Canadian," Shawna said.

Greta said, "That's true. Your parents aren't, though."

"Yes, they are." She was getting a tone.

"You're right. They are. I only meant they weren't born here, that's all."

TJ said, "Let's see... Oliver's Canadian. And Wayne, in apartment number one. Was Emma born here?"

"She was. So that's what, four out eleven?" Greta decided to let TJ's misdemeanors go for the time being. She made a mental note to think up an excuse to leave her at home next week.

TJ said, "No, it's five out of twelve but two of them are our kids. Baby Tony was born here, too, remember. Everybody else is from the states."

After thinking about it, Greta said, "I wonder if it's because of where we're situated. There's that big truck stop up north a ways and on the other side of the highway, what's it called?"

"Knight of the Road?" TJ said.

"Yeah. People driving south would already be in Canada and would be likely to stop at that one instead. Maybe."

TJ said, "A lot of us did just kinda blow in off the highway. I mean, it's not like there's much reason to move here deliberately."

"This is the best place to live!"

Greta said, "I know, sweetie. It's a wonderful place to live." That seemed to mollify Shawna. She started making motorboat noises at Emma, who giggled and tried to do it back.

Women and kids were still settling in when they arrived at Montie's house in Fireweed City. Greta was relieved to see that they weren't too awful late this time. It was Montie's turn to host the mother's circle. At the first meeting, last week, there were about a dozen women with their babies and pre-schoolers, at a woman's house over in Morton. Greta guessed some of them must be driving in from some distance away. She didn't see last week's hostess here today.

The mothers sat in a big circle around the room. The kids played with toys, at the center of the circle of mothers. Last week, they'd gone around the room in rounds, answering questions the hostess asked. One of the first questions was to tell a fun fact about yourself. Most of the revelations weren't very interesting. But then, who would want to reveal anything too juicy to a bunch of strangers.

Greta hit it off with Montie right away last week. Montie's fun fact was that her real name was Monticello. She seemed quite normal, for someone with parents who gave her such a weird name. When Greta's turn came around, she'd had a wild urge to tell them about the imaginary friend her husband carried around in his shirt pocket. But she told them that she liked to make soap, though she'd only made it once, at the time.

Now Greta said, "Hi Montie. Thanks so much for having us. Hope you don't mind too much, my neighbor here jumped into my car." She hoped the face she made, along with her words, would give Montie the appropriate message.

Montie laughed a little, uneasy. Shawna took a big blueberry muffin from the snack table and started eating it, though snacks hadn't been offered yet. Greta hoped she'd get a minute alone with Montie, so she could explain that Shawna had literally jumped into car and that she'd been afraid to try to get her out.

Wait, no. Some of these ladies were real helicopters. Greta could just see them nattering on about how she'd brought a dangerous lunatic around their babies. Well, Shawna might be a lunatic, sort of, but she wasn't dangerous. It was more like she was just one more small child, only in a larger size. Maybe it would be better to just hope the whole thing would be forgotten. She gave Montie a hostess gift, three bars of lemon soap that she'd made especially for the occasion, tied with a pretty ribbon.

"Oh! Did you make these?" Montie remembered Greta's personal fun fact.

Greta nodded, hoping that it would earn her some forgiveness about Shawna. She tried not to look too proud of the soap, though the batch did turn out nice. It smelled like a lemon dessert, luscious enough to eat. Greta said, "TJ's gone back to the car for my cookies." Each week, they were to sign up for the snack they'd bring the following week. Greta wanted be sure Montie knew that she'd brought homemade nut butter cookies, as promised. TJ only signed up to bring a bag of potato chips, then forgot about it.

TJ and Shawna made Greta think of an assembly she'd had go to back in high school. It happened to be about the dangers of recreational drugs. The presenter had used the example of a pot of live crabs on the stove, to illustrate what happened when you got in with the wrong crowd. Even though the water was heating up, when you tried to get out, the other crabs would keep reaching up with their pinchers and trying to pull you back down to your doom. There was no dope involved in this situation (as far as Greta knew) but TJ and Shawna were definitely yanking her back hard, into the pot of only having doofuses for friends.

Montie had arranged sofas and folding chairs for the group, hugging her living room walls. Blankets were spread out on the carpet in the middle of the room, with toys scattered about for the kids. It was like last week at that other chick's house, only this time they got to sit on furniture instead of the floor.

After they were all seated, Montie started by asking the new ladies to tell something about themselves, and to include a personal fun fact. Montie's son was three like Emma. Their kids had played together well last week. So far, Montie was Greta's first pick to befriend, though she wasn't sure how to go about it, beyond making small talk when the opportunity arose. Asking Montie to go do something together seemed kind of creepy, kind of like asking her out on a date. Greta tried to remember how she made friends when she was young, single and childless. She'd had a lot of friends then but she didn't remember doing anything special to get them. Back then, friendships just happened.

She watched for chances to be helpful. One of the new girls looked very young. She had a precious, month-old girl in an adorable outfit with pink hearts all over it. The girl's fun fact was that she collected hearts. She pointed out her baby's outfit as proof, then added that she owned glass hearts, ceramic hearts, wall art hearts and heart boxes. She had many heart-shaped items in her bedroom at her parents' home, where she lived with her baby. Greta was glad she wasn't a single mother who had to live with her parents.

The next newcomer was about as different from the first new girl as possible. She had one-year-old twin girls from China. She was 44 years old, a licensed real estate agent, though she mostly stayed home with her babies now. She and her husband tried to conceive for a decade before adopting. Her fun fact was that she'd just found out she was twelve-point-five percent Black, from one of those recreational mail order DNA tests. There was an awkward silence.

The woman looked around with a weak smile, like she realized she'd made a faux pas but wasn't sure what it was. Greta guessed the silence was because the woman had mentioned race rather than country. The woman seemed to guess that too. She tried again. "I was twelve-point-five percent Sub-Sahara African, about one third German-French and the rest was mostly southern Italian." She looked around again, like she was checking to see if she'd been exonerated.

Greta, at only thirty-two, had found herself on the wrong side of the ever-changing rules of social correctness more than once. She felt for the woman and tried to smooth over the awkwardness by moving the discussion on to this week's last newbie. "And here's Shawna. She lives in my building in Nomads Nest."

A beak-nosed girl said, incredulously, "You mean... You live at the truck stop?" It didn't sound very nice at all.

Greta said, "Yes," in a small voice. She looked down meekly, hoping to court sympathy from the others, subtly signaling that Beak-nose had been unkind. But TJ and Shawna ruined her chance at sympathy.

TJ had somehow managed to push her way in between Greta and Montie. She'd just picked up her folding chair and wedged it right in there. Then TJ turned to Montie, blocking Greta from the conversation, and butting in on the introduction. She loudly complimented Montie on her long, wavy hairstyle. Montie replied that she was a beautician, that she did hair in her kitchen. Greta felt a twinge of jealousy. She hadn't known Montie did hair. TJ flipped her own hair back then. It was almost like TJ was flirting with Montie, Greta thought.

Shawna looked up from the floor, where she stacked big plastic blocks, as much as one could stack blocks on a carpet topped with blankets. She said, "I'm Shawna and I'm pregnant." She looked around the room with an expectant smile, like she'd just told a hilarious joke. Greta pictured Shawna using the same method to present the news to Karen. But Karen knew Shawna's tricks better than anybody. Karen would probably just ignore her.

The beak-nosed chick was still at it. Like the evil witch who acts syrupy sweet in the fairy tales, she said, "Oh, congratulations! Are you and your baby's father married?" Who would ask someone that?

Shawna put a block on top of her creation and it all fell down, causing her face to redden in anger. She said, "My baby's father is married but I'm not!"

There was a collective gasp. Shawna seemed pleased with the attention. She brightened up, announcing, "That's my fun fact."

Greta had a terrifying thought. If it was true, who was the father? *Could it be Max?*

No. Not her Max. Greta didn't think Max found Shawna at all attractive, even if Greta did think he'd cheat, which she didn't. But could anyone ever say *not my husband,* with 100% certainty?

The color drained from TJ's face. She looked at Greta conspiratorially, like *do you believe this shit?*

Oh, *now* she remembers I exist, Greta thought. But why would TJ care, even if… She'd left Oliver anyway. It might be a respect thing though, since Shawna was supposed to be TJ's friend. Yeah, that would piss anyone off. Ah right, there was also child support to consider. Oliver didn't make much money. If he had to pay for another kid, that would leave even less for TJ. Or maybe TJ wasn't thinking about any of that but was just shocked like everyone else in the room.

Shawna had said she was pregnant in the car, but they hadn't paid much attention. It had seemed like Shawna just wanted an excuse to go out with her and TJ. But maybe it was true.

Nomads Nest was pretty isolated, especially for people who didn't drive, like Shawna. Shawna might take the bus once in a while but Greta wasn't even sure about that. She usually only saw Shawna leave the building with Karen or Jack. And she'd never known Shawna to have a boyfriend. So, on the outside chance Shawna's news was true, she'd guess Oliver would be the father. Besides Max and Oliver, there were only the three old men in the building: Wayne and Tony. And, of course, Shawna's dad, who Greta didn't even want to consider. Well, there was a steady stream of people stopping in off the highway, for gas and snacks.

But customers didn't usually stick around, so she'd still put her money on Oliver, if she was even going to entertain the notion that it could be true.

She didn't have to wonder about it for long. Beak-nose, coming in for the kill said, innocently, "Oh, really? What's his name?"

Shawna said, "Oliver." Just straight out said it.

Almost immediately, TJ was on top of Shawna, beating the crap out of her. Or would have been anyway, if Shawna wasn't twice TJ's size.

Neither of them knew how to fight. TJ was kinda gonging Shawna's head, rhythmically boxing her ears.

Shawna seemed to have picked up TJ's dual hand approach. From her position, on her back on the floor, she repeatedly slapped TJ's face with both hands at once, like she was playing pattycake on it.

The other women yelled, snatched up babies, and rushed away from the action, or else closer to it. Total pandemonium. A stray leg from the TJ-Shawna pile made contact with Montie's son, and knocked him down. Oh no, no, no.

He screamed his head off. Montie picked him up, rocked him and patted his back. His yells calmed to whimpers. She hissed, "You three. Get out. Now."

Greta gathered up Emma and slunk towards the door but it didn't seem like TJ and Shawna even heard Montie. Shawna was on top now and appeared to be doing the pattycake thing on TJ's face from a different angle. TJ snapped at Shawna's hands with her mouth, like a dog. It was all so fucked up that Greta start laughing. She couldn't stop.

Montie said, "You think it's funny, bitch? Well, you'll be rolling with laughter soon then, because I'm calling the cops." She handed her kid off to Beak-nose, who eagerly stood by, ready to assist. Montie pushed buttons on her phone.

Beak-nose said, "You're goddamn right," apparently Montie's new bestie, all sanctimonious, though she really started it all.

Greta rushed to TJ and Shawna and tried to yank them apart. She shouted, "Cops. Are. Coming. Let's. Go!"

That got their attention. TJ gathered up baby Tony and ran for the door. Shawna stopped at the snack table to shovel treats into her purse on the way out.

Behind them, Beak-nose said, "Truck stop trash." Someone else said, "Not our type, ladies."

Montie said, "Yeah, that was insane. We need to start a screening process."

A chorus of "Yeah" and "Mmm-hmm" followed Greta out the door.

Jiminy fucking Christmas. The public humiliation would no doubt follow Greta throughout her daughter's school years. She'd probably lost all chance of having a normal friend here. And she still had to put up with Beavis and Butthead on the ride home.

She turned on Adele, with the volume up as loud as she dared, considering the tender baby eardrums among them.

She hummed along, adding her own words. "When We Were Young (Crabs)." "Rolling in the Deep (Crab Pot)." "Set Fire to the (Crab Pot) Rain."

By the time they were a few miles from home, TJ and Shawna had made up. They cracked jokes about it, mimicking the other women's reactions.

They shared stolen pastries from Shawna's purse and didn't even offer any to Greta. Greta thought about pulling over and ordering them out of her car. Maybe she'd honk her horn continuously as they walked down the road. But then, they probably wouldn't get out. She just kept driving.

Tulpamancy

Lonnie's phone rang, jerking her mind from the movie script she was writing, which featured herself in the starring role. In it, she was a mistreated young wife and mother, Suki Sullivan, who would slip away from her evil husband and hide in the drainage sewer tunnel near their suburban home. From there, she'd listen to the developing horrors that went on in their house, with the aid of a baby monitor. Lonnie was so deeply immersed in the scene of Suki in the sewer that the interruption felt to her like being yanked out of bed in the middle of the night. She wasn't going to answer it but then she saw Greta's name on her phone. If you didn't answer, goddamn Greta was liable to show up at your door.

Greta said, "Hey, girl. Are you out of Shawna's hearing range? Watch her, girl. Her and TJ getting us kicked out of the mother's group, Jiminy Christmas. I wouldn't put anything past either one of them anymore."

The first time Greta told her the story, Lonnie howled with laughter. But Greta didn't see the humor. Greta was all furious because they'd ruined her chance to make boring friends at the snobby mothers' group. This was the third time she'd called Lonnie to rant about it, not even bothering to say hello first.

Lonnie took a pack of chicken tenders out of the freezer. She'd rather hang out with TJ and Shawna than the goofy moms. She said, "Well, anybody could get in a fight, given the right circumstances." Greta huffed into the phone. Lonnie stifled a giggle.

"Grown women. One a mother and the other pregnant. Getting into a violent, physical altercation with each other. In someone's home! Not to mention, children witnessed this. You think that's okay now, really?"

Lonnie didn't care about it. She decided to take another little poke at Greta. "I wouldn't say it's *okay*. But forgivable. As long as it's only once in a while."

There was a long silence. Greta irritated her, acting like hitting someone automatically made you Dirty Dingus McGee until your dying day. Karen had forgiven Lonnie for the misunderstanding in the attic, for example. They'd moved past it right away. Karen didn't hype it all up and make Lonnie out to be some evil nutcase from outer space over it.

Lonnie changed the subject. She said, "To answer your question, Shawna's at Karen's." She didn't tell Greta that Shawna wasn't pregnant after all. It wasn't any of Greta's business. Lonnie had gotten a bit protective of Shawna. It was almost like Shawna was her kid sister or something. Her booby prize kid sister, since she doubted she'd get to see her real one again anytime soon.

After becoming roommates with Shawna and becoming friends with Karen, she'd learned that Shawna was slower, mentally, than you might notice at first. Knowing Shawna's limitations made it obvious that Oliver took advantage of her. Slick, slippery Oliver. Olive oil. He was at the root of it all but Greta never even mentioned him.

Greta said, "The reason I'm calling is--- this is between you and me only, okay, sweetie? And please hear me out."

"Um. Okay." She fidgeted with the frozen chicken tenders, arranging them on a plate. She stuck the plate into the microwave, on "defrost." Greta's hemming and hawing was what people did when they were trying to rope you into something. She put water on the stove to boil for the noodles. Now she just had to decide on a vegetable.

"Max and I are going to a two-day tulpas meeting this weekend. I was wondering if you'd come along, partly as a babysitter and partly as a friend. I'd pay your way."

"What? Tulips?"

"Tul-pas. It's a long story, girl. Are you busy? Can I come over?"

"Um, sure. Okay." She regretted it as soon as it slipped out of her mouth. She was kind of jealous of Greta. She'd thought she was headed for having what Greta had, a decent husband, and then, a child. But it was cruelly yanked away from her. Greta had it all and didn't appreciate it. Besides, she was pushy.

Lonnie rushed around tidying the place, annoyed that she cared what Greta thought of the state of her apartment. Then she started peeling carrots at the kitchen table. Maybe Greta wouldn't stay long when she saw that Lonnie was getting ready for dinner.

There was a tap on the door, then Greta was in her apartment. She didn't wait for Lonnie to answer the door. "Hey," she said, setting Emma down.

"Um, there you are. Hi Emma! How are you, cutie-pie?" Lonnie got a pot out from under the sink and showed Emma how to drum on it with a spoon. Then she silently chided herself, since that was kind of signaling that she expected more than a momentary visit.

Greta sat down on the sofa. She said, "I can trust you, can't I?"

This again. Lonnie said, "Yes. You can trust me. Now what's up?"

"Max has a kind of… unusual problem."

Lonnie motioned for her to continue. She'd stopped her dinner preparations and moved into the living room, which was more annoyance. But it seemed rude to stay in the kitchen after Greta made herself comfortable in the living room. Why did the rude people always seem to get their way? Max having an unusual problem sounded interesting, though. Perhaps Max claimed he was captured by aliens and used for medical experiments in their spaceship. Or maybe he could only get it up if Greta took an ice cold bath first, then lay very, very still.

Greta said, "Max has a tulpa."

"What's a tulpa? Is it like a FUPA?" Lonnie snickered. Greta glared. Emma didn't bang on the pot. She stirred pretend food in it, talking softly to herself about making candy. She was so adorable. Lonnie could just swoop her up. "Soory," she said.

Greta nodded, reluctantly. "This is serious, okay? Anyway, a tulpa is an alter ego. You know, what someone with a dissociative disorder might have, only nowhere near as bad."

"Whoa. Multiple personalities?"

"No! Nothing even remotely that drastic. He *knows* it's not real, sort of. It's similar to... an imaginary friend."

"Oh. How do you spell it?"

"T-u-l-p-a. It's included in eastern spirituality and all that. It was a big fad a few years back, so I'm surprised you haven't heard of it."

Lonnie thought Greta was trying hard to make this weirdness sound less weird. She said, "Hold on. My water's boiling." In the kitchen, she put the noodles into the boiling water, then set the timer on her phone.

When she returned, Greta said, "The meeting's in a hotel in Calgary, on Saturday and Sunday. We'll pay for everything, as long as you're okay with all four of us in one room? You'd share a bed with Emma, of course. You'd just have to watch her for me, whenever it's needed. If nothing else, it's a change of scenery, right?"

"Hmm. Are they going to cure him?"

"I hope so, girl. I mean, not that he's mentally ill or anything. But it's just too different. You know? And sometimes I think he's closer to Min than he is to me. Min is the tulpa's name."

"Ah, got it." This was interesting as hell. She'd never met an adult who had an imaginary friend. She said, "So, we'd be back by Monday morning for sure?" Lonnie's living expenses were so low right now that she'd been able to take it easy, which she had really, really needed. She helped an elderly couple who used to live in this building, three days a week. Wayne set her up with them, after he'd made her apologize for laughing at Shawna's Wayne, Wayne, water brain joke. Lonnie stayed in Fireweed City from Monday mornings until Wednesday nights. With such low rent and no car expenses, she made enough to get by on.

Greta said, "It's all day Saturday and all day Sunday. We'll drive down Saturday morning and come back Sunday evening. We'll only stay over on Saturday night. I'm hoping to get this tulpa mess over and done with. I'll tell you, it's about to drive me over the edge."

Lonnie knew about nearly being driven over the edge. She said, "That sucks. All right. I'll come." The timer went off. Lonnie said, "Oops, I've got to get back to my noodles." She hoped Greta would take the hint and go home.

"Perfect. And thanks, Lonnie. I appreciate it. And remember, this is ---"

"Just between us. Got it," Lonnie called from the kitchen. She looked forward to Saturday but she wanted to get back to what she was doing for now. She decided to stay in the kitchen until Greta left. She finished peeling and cutting up the carrots. She poured oil in a pan to sauté' the chicken in.

Greta stuck her head in. "We've gotta go. See you Saturday. Seven a.m."

"I'll be here."

When dinner was ready, she fixed a plate for Shawna and put it in the fridge, then sat down to eat. Between bites, she did an internet search:

Tulpa: A thought-form created in the mind that becomes sentient, with thoughts, feelings and memories independent of its creator.

It sounded like the main character in the script she was writing, who constantly did things that Lonnie didn't see coming at all. She picked up her phone. "Karen? You got a minute? Listen, Greta was just here and you're not gonna believe this shit…"

#

Riding in the backseat of Max and Greta's car, Lonnie felt sad about not having a car herself anymore, about always having to wait for the bus. But her next thought was that when she had a car, she couldn't have four-day weekends.

She wondered if that thought could be considered to be coming from a voice inside her head. If so, she guessed all she'd have to do was pay a lot more attention to that voice, and she could grow it into its very own person. She wasn't sure if that was a fascinating thought or just a dumb one. Emma chirped, "Cat!" and Lonnie told her no, that was a dog, that the lady on the sidewalk was walking on a leash. "Doggie?" Emma said.

"Okay, close enough." There were large, magnificent dogs everywhere in Alberta. Husky-ish, blue-eyed, Arctic dogs.

At the hotel, the front desk clerk was snippy. She refused to let them check in until one o'clock sharp, so they hung out in the lobby, drinking free coffee and whispering about what a bitch the front desk clerk was. Max started explaining tulpas to Lonnie, but Greta shushed him.

Greta handed Lonnie the car keys at a few minutes before nine, and she and Max left for their tulpa meeting in the hotel's conference room.

Driving again after three months felt strange. Lonnie wasn't sure enough of herself to get on the freeway, so she stayed on the main road that ran in front of the hotel. She pulled in at a Tim Hortons but only got a small order of assorted Timbits, to share with Emma. Greta didn't give her any money, which made her mad, since Greta had said she'd pay for everything. Did she expect Lonnie to just drive Emma around for hours? After Tim Hortons, Lonnie spotted a park from the road. She took Emma to play on the playground equipment.

When Emma finally tired of sliding and swinging, they drove down the main road some more, and found a Walmart. Some woman there made a sharp remark to Lonnie about Emma playing with the toys. Trucks, balls and dolls were in bins, unpackaged, at kid-height in the toy aisles. Therefore, Lonnie assumed they wanted the kids to play with the toys, hoping the parents would then buy the toys. Either way, she was upset over the sharp scolding. She just wanted to leave.

Back in the Walmart parking lot, she wondered if the woman, who was alone, was jealous, seeing Lonnie with cute little Emma. Lonnie certainly knew that feeling herself. Not that it made the woman's behavior okay. It just seemed to Lonnie that when someone hit you with such a strong slap of unexpected vitriol, there was likely a personal problem behind it. The thought soothed her a bit, anyway.

They arrived back at the hotel early because Lonnie was out of low-cost ideas for keeping a three-year-old entertained on the streets of Calgary. Greta was in the lobby, alone, in the same chair she'd sat in that morning. Her eyes were red, as if she'd been crying.

Lonnie said, "What's wrong?"

"Nothing. Everything. Let's go to lunch, girl. I need to think."

Lonnie handed her the car keys and took Emma's hand. On the way back to the car, she said, "Max isn't coming?"

"Max can have his lunch with Min. And then he can marry her."

"Oh. His tulpa is a 'she?'"

"Yes."

At McDonald's, Greta asked Lonnie to watch Emma, while she went to the counter to order. She came back with a kiddie meal for Emma. And a regular hamburger, small fries and Coke for each of them, from the dollar menu. Lonnie made a mental note to not help her out again. She knew Greta paid TJ five bucks an hour to babysit. And here she wouldn't even buy Lonnie a decent fast food lunch, when she was only paying for Lonnie to sleep in a room Greta would have to pay for anyway.

Greta said, "I thought this meeting was about trying to cure Max's problem. It's not. It's to celebrate it and learn how to do more of it."

"Whoa. Was it a misunderstanding?"

"No girl, it was a fucking lie. He says he thought I'd finally understand, if I heard more about it. He said the topic has become so heated between us that he wanted me to hear the stories of other tulpamancers, to try to get me to understand. That's what he called them, "tulpamancers." It sounds like 'necromancers,' doesn't it? I think it's sick. I am tired of having to compete with a mistress who isn't even real." She started crying again. Lonnie grappled for something to say.

"Well, if you don't think it's real anyway, could you maybe just try to ignore it?"

"If I don't *think* it's real? Do you think it's real, Lonnie?"

"I don't know."

Greta narrowed her eyes. "Of course it's not real. That's just stupid. But I'm still left sitting there by myself, like I'm a leper or something. He completely ignores me. Too busy blowing kisses into his shirt pocket."

"Cookie!" Emma said, delighted to find one in her kiddie meal carton.

Lonnie said, "Aren't you a lucky ducky! Here, let me open the package for you."

Greta said, "And then. Girl, the people at that meeting. It reminded me of a documentary I saw once about a prison for the criminally insane. Wall to wall weirdos. I just don't know if I can continue on with him."

I could. The thought popped into Lonnie's mind out of nowhere, as if it came from a tulpa. It shocked her. First of all, she barely knew Max and had barely ever even noticed him. Second, Greta was her friend. Sort of. Third, Lonnie wasn't a trash pile like the ex-friend in her past, She Whose Name Shall Not Be Spoken. She slipped a couple of Greta's French fries out of their paper holder and into her mouth. Ah, that was it. She was just mad at Greta for being stingy, when Lonnie was doing her a favor. That was all.

She wouldn't mind stopping by the tulpa meeting herself, as long as they were there anyway. She wouldn't doubt that where Greta saw criminal mental patients, she might see creative introverts. The whole idea intrigued her, suddenly. Two spirits sharing one body, wow. As she got back into the car, she tried to think of how to ask if she could take Greta's place at the meeting, if Greta didn't want to go back to it.

But when they got back to the turn-off into the hotel parking lot, Greta kept driving. She didn't say anything and neither did Lonnie, until they were back on the highway, headed home.

On the Way Home

"Ready for our date, babe?" Jack said. It was the last day of the month, Jack and Karen's customary business meeting day.

"Oh, shut up," she said. He'd donned his Hawaiian shirt and gold chain, splashed on Armani. He tried to get romance credit for their monthly business meetings, just because it was only the two of them and they were held in restaurants. They didn't get out much, so having their monthly meetings in restaurants was an incentive for them to have monthly meetings at all. But there was nothing romantic about it. It wasn't a damn date.

"Ah, hate is the most passionate love! Nom, nom!" He kissed his way up her arm, making slobbery sucking noises.

"You romantic old dog, you." She managed to free herself, then gathered up the folder and notes she'd prepared. She liked the formality of printing out reports the old way, instead of dragging their laptops along with them.

They were on the highway before either of them remembered that they didn't know where they were headed. He said, "The buffet in Fireweed City again?"

"I was thinking we could try that new barbecue joint in Morton, Ray's Ribs?"

"Yes, ma'am."

"You better call me ma'am, boy."

"Uh-uh. Don't ever call a Black man 'boy.'"

"Oh. Sorry. Girl."

"I am ignoring you. Oh, look at that smoke. Another track fire."

When it was as dry as it was now in late July, sparks from the train wheels turning on the rails started little fires in the surrounding brush. Sometimes they spread. She said, "I got it," and dialed the fire department. The dispatcher said that others had already called. But you never knew. She always called them in.

They rode along for a while, listening to Lady Gaga. Karen had downloaded it because she was on a kick to catch up with the times. She'd heard Lady Gaga's name a lot but had no idea what her songs were. She'd finally gotten around to reading the first Harry Potter book just last week. She didn't see what all the fuss was about with that, either. She said, "This happens too often now, these fires. And they can get out of control quick. Couldn't they just clear away the brush alongside the tracks?"

"Hmm. It seems like they could. Turn here?"

"Yes." They didn't start their monthly meeting until after they ordered lunch. Like so many of their marital habits, she didn't remember when or why that unspoken rule started.

They had to wait a few minutes for the restaurant to open. They always tried to arrive by the eleven o'clock opening times, so they won't feel harried. Hogging a table when the lunch rush was in full swing after 12:30 or so wasn't ideal for anyone.

They both got the salad with shredded barbecued chicken on top. Fork food, not finger food, since Karen didn't want barbecue sauce on their documents. But they agreed to come back another time and try the ribs. Of course, alcoholic beverages were mandatory. These days, that was a special perk that you had to own your own business to get. She remembered when employees everywhere were allowed alcoholic beverages at lunch.

First, they went over costs, profits and miscellaneous for the fueling part of the business. Then they did the convenience store. She said, "So, the last inventory shows that quite a lot of stock went missing, mainly baby items. Formula, baby food, Pampers."

"Yeah. I checked the security cameras but they were already recorded over. They only showed the past few days, which didn't show any theft. The picture's real fuzzy anyway. I'm looking at updating the whole system but the good ones are expensive." She wrote a note: *New security cameras being considered.*

She said, "TJ's the only one in the building with a baby. But I think he's past formula age, isn't he? I don't remember when formula ends anymore. I'll check and see what size Pampers are missing, too. That might be a clue. I doubt TJ would suddenly start stealing baby stuff though, especially now that her father's helping her. Eh, it's probably some druggie again, taking baby items to re-sell. Can you bring it up with Oliver? He might have some idea of who'd be doing it."

"There, you see? He's a valuable employee."

"That's not the issue, though. Anyway, we'll get around to that rat bastard soon enough."

They proceeded to the "Apartments" section of the meeting. They went through them by number. "Apartment number one," she said, after another sip of Caesar cocktail. "Woo! The drinks are strong today."

"Yes, ma'am. Number one, Wayne's place. No problems there. Next?"

Wayne was never a problem. She wished they were all like him. She swallowed a mouthful of barbecued chicken. "Maybe we don't need to come back here for the ribs. This deep in cattle country, you'd think they'd learn how to barbecue."

"It's all right."

"That's the thing, though. It's always just 'all right.' In cattle country, the barbecue should be great. It should be fabulous."

Jack said, "I think it's got to do with the type of local wood that's available to cook over."

"Interesting." She took another sip of her drink. "This drink is excellent. Strong, though. I'm feeling a little tipsy already. Okay, apartment number two. Oliver. It's high time we got rid of the bastard."

Jack groaned. "Come on now. Don't start that again. He pays his rent on time and he's a rock solid employee. We can't afford to get rid of the bastard."

"He is a perverted bastard."

"No, he's not. He's just a regular, everyday bastard. If we got rid of people based on that alone, we wouldn't have any renters, employees *or* customers."

"Or husbands."

It came out harsher than Karen intended but Jack seemed to find being called a bastard highly amusing. He ordered a second round of Caesar cocktails, as if in celebration.

She said, "Well no, you're not a bastard at all, hon. But you know, this whole thing, there's nothing funny about it. He knows about Shawna's… limitations, but it didn't stop him. Shawna is very vulnerable. She trusts everybody and just wants everybody to like her. He's a creep. A predator."

"And I'm gonna stick with my position that it was a very grey area. If you think Shawna is that vulnerable, then we need to watch her a hell of a lot more closely. We can't let her out there just like everybody else, then start ruining people's lives when they treat her just like everybody else. Anyway, I have spoken to him. He gave me his word that it won't happen again. I believe him, since he's been put on notice that he'll lose his job *and* his apartment if it does. Now, I consider the matter closed."

"Cheesecake!" Karen shrieked at the waiter. "I mean, may I have a slice of cheesecake? No topping please, just plain."

"Now remember, you wanted me to help you stay on your diet. Does stress eating help your diet?"

"Yes." She wrote in her notebook: Oliver- Discussion to be continued.

Jack said, "Okay, now. Apartment number three?"

Jack was always sure to include their apartment number in the rundown. He thought he was quite funny. She said, "There have been far too many complaints about a huge, odiferous male dog in that unit. His name is... Well, they'd only say that it starts with a "J" and ends with a "K." He incessantly lifts his leg and sprays the residents. I'm afraid he'll have to go."

"I'm the dog, right?"

"I'm afraid so." She made him toast to it. "Next up, number four- TJ and the Tonys."

"TJ and the Tonys. Sounds like they should be in concert. Let's see. Tony reported a dripping kitchen faucet and a couple of other little things. All fixed. Do you have the completed work orders and receipts?"

"Got 'em." It was (usually) encouraging when a renter reported minor problems. It let her know they cared about the place.

Jack said, "How come you don't want to kick that TJ girl out? Why only Oliver? From what I hear, TJ definitely physically assaulted Shawna."

"No-no. I'm glad she did it. That falls under the category of 'a life lesson,' to stay away from married men."

"Never thought I'd hear you take anybody else's side, when it comes to them versus your Shawna."

"Uh-huh, when she's a problem, she's *my* Shawna. Eh, the girls have made up now, anyway. Besides, in case you didn't notice, *my* Shawna won the fight. Did you see TJ's fat split lip? Ha-ha. Okay, next up is number five- Max and Greta. That's a bit of a dicey situation. Lonnie said Max moved out. You know, because of the pocket pal?"

Jack started humming "Imaginary Lover." He made her toast to it.

"So. We shouldn't be surprised if Greta doesn't have the rent next month or breaks the lease or whatever. Got it." She wrote: *Keep an eye on apartment number five.* "Here, finish this cheesecake, would you, hon? I'm on a diet, you know."

Jack was so eager for the tiny sliver of remaining dessert that he hard-snatched it, making the fork flip onto the floor.

"Can't take you anywhere," she joked, retrieving the sticky utensil from the carpet. She said, "Now for the last apartment- drum roll, please- number six. Shawna and Lonnie."

Jack said, "Did you do that photo inventory we talked about, of all the stuff in there that's from the attic?"

"Nah, I decided not to bother. I really doubt Lonnie would steal from us and that old junk's not worth anything anyway. You should see how clean that place is, by the way. Lonnie says she and Shawna usually clean and cook together. Shawna listens to her."

"Excellent. Are we done with the apartments section, then?"

"Yes. But there is something I wanted to talk to you about, as long as we're on the topic of Shawna. I think we should get her sterilized. Or whatever it's called now."

Jack said, "Well. That sounds severe. But, you definitely have a point."

"Ever since she thought she was pregnant, she's been obsessed with pregnancy and babies, you know. We'll be lucky to get her to a level where she's able to just take care of herself."

"How would you go about it, though? Shawna won't like it."

"Well, I was thinking about calling my doctor. To see if I can get her to talk to Shawna. Shawna might listen to a doctor, you know?"

"Worth a try, I guess." He drained his glass. "It also sounds like it might be a clue in the missing baby items caper."

"Oh, stop. Shawna wouldn't steal. One more thing. I've been thinking about the attic, how we could make it into another apartment. Or we could, I don't know, do something else with it. I'm not in a hurry about it, though."

Jack said, "Hmm. Okay, I'll think that over."

On the way home, they killed somebody.

They started bickering about Oliver again in the car. Just then, a goose landed on the highway in front of them. Jack swerved to miss the goose, and he ran into a girl who was walking down the side of road, on that lonely stretch of highway.

They both rushed out of the car to render aid but the girl was just gone. Dead. A young, impoverished looking Native girl with a ratty red backpack. Karen couldn't bear to look anymore. She turned away.

Her survival instincts kicked in. They were likely both legally intoxicated. Their drinks had probably been double the strength they'd expected. It certainly had felt like it. Until now. Now she felt entirely sober. "Don't touch anything!" she said. "Let's go."

Jack looked all around him. He stood there, looking and looking and kind of flapping his arms.

She pushed him toward the car and that's when they heard it. A high-pitched, weak wail.

"A baby! Fucking hell, Jack. Get in the car!"

She hurried over to the baby, a tiny thing, swooped it up, then dashed back to the car.

"Okay, hon. Now just drive slow and steady. Slow and steady. We just need to get home and then everything will be all right. Just get home."

It was a nightmare. Each time the infant made its thin wail, she thought she'd leave her body.

Jack already had one drunk driving conviction, from years ago. Another, combined with... this, and he'd be toast. *They'd* be toast. Well. The poor girl was dead. Nothing more could be done for her anyway. They needed to cover this up. Nothing had ever been more clear to her in her life.

Finally, finally, they were in their usual spot in the truck stop parking lot.

"Turn off the car, Jack." His face was expressionless, mask-like.

She said, "Okay hon, now get me one of those big grocery totes from the trunk. Please."

He did. She maneuvered the baby into the bag. She said, "We're going up to the attic, okay? You go first. If you see or hear anyone, yell, 'Karen, do you have my keys?' Okay? I'm gonna play music on my phone to try and drown out any cries."

Mercifully, they made it to the attic undetected. Then the baby started its small cries again. Jack started unfreezing, coming back into himself. He said, "Don't worry, babe. Nobody'll hear that. This is northern construction. The insulation is very thick."

She exhaled, relieved. "I know this sounds horrible, considering... but I need a drink."

"Oh, I feel you, babe."

"Can you go down and get us a bottle? Whatever's in the pantry. And we'll need some formula, newborn Pampers and... never mind, I'll go. Can you hold it, I mean, er, him or her, until I get back?"

Jack took the baby. He got up and paced, patting its back.

When Karen entered the store downstairs, Oliver said, "Hello, Mrs. Shay."

God, she hated him. Still running on instinct, she said, "Sweep the back room, right away. I've heard through the grapevine that we might be getting a surprise inspection."

"Really? Is it a fire inspection or... what?"

"I don't know. Hurry up."

He slithered into the back room and she quickly filled the shopping tote, with merchandise this time: Pampers, wipes, ready-made formula, a pacifier and the only baby bottle left on the shelves.

She stopped at their apartment for a bottle of wine and the corkscrew, then decided to bring her laptop and mouse.

Back in the attic, she still wasn't entirely sure that she wasn't having some terrible dream.

She opened the wine, took a long drink out of the bottle. Jack passed the baby to her and she passed the wine to him. She said, "All right. Now, let me get this baby taken care of for the moment. And then we can settle in and think this through. Can you look up those places where you can drop off babies anonymously? My laptop's in the bag."

Jack searched the internet while she poured formula into the bottle and fed the baby. The poor little thing was ravenous. She realized then that she hadn't washed the new bottle before using it. The baby was so small and fragile that she feared any stray germs might be enough to do it in. The baby gazed at her with those dark eyes like it was searching her soul. It seemed to say, *Where's Mother? When is Mother coming back?* She was relieved when its eyes closed. Poor little thing.

Jack read aloud about an anonymous infant drop-off place. The closest one was about an hour and a half drive away.

But she'd noticed something that changed everything. She said, "Jack, we can't."

He took another swig from the bottle, then looked at her quizzically.

"See how this space between this little one's nose and mouth is smooth, how it doesn't have the typical vertical indentation? That's fetal alcohol syndrome." Shawna was only considered borderline or mildly disabled but Karen had still picked up a lot about special needs children in general, through the years.

"We can't what?"

She said, "We can't drop it off. Who would adopt a disabled baby? Nobody, most likely. And we took this one's mother away."

"What are you trying to say?"

"This little angel is our responsibility now."

"Are you crazy?"

"Hush a sec, please. Let me think." She remembered a couple of old rocking chairs from when she cleaned up here. Lonnie took one and left the other. She asked Jack to bring it over. In the meantime, she changed the baby. It was a boy. He didn't appear to be injured, surprisingly. A small piece of umbilical cord was still attached. He couldn't be more than a few days old.

#

Karen had been at the hotel in Kamloops with the baby for a couple of hours when Jack called, at ten p.m. He'd driven Shawna separately, to an Airbnb nearby. Their cover story was simple, that they'd just decided to get away for a while before the summer was over. Her instincts had screamed at her to get out of town, so here they were. Her instincts were reinforced when she saw the evening news story about a young Native woman's body, found along the highway near Morton.

"Did you do it yet?" she said into the phone.

"Yes. She's out like a rock." She'd given him an old bottle of Percocet, left over from some dental work she'd had done a couple of years earlier.

"You'll stay up and keep an eye on her, right?"

"Of course."

"If she wakes up before I get there, give her some more."

"Yes ma'am."

"Sorry. I know you already know that. I'm just anxious. Are you doing okay?"

"Well, I'm still breathing. How about you?"

"Yeah, we're fine. Well, I guess I'll get to bed now. It's been a day. Talk to you at... about five in the morning?"

"All right. And Karen?"

"Yes?"

"Thank you. A million times, thank you."

"You're quite welcome, hon. 'Night."

"Goodnight."

She cradled the baby on the hotel bed, in the dimmed lights, humming "Rockabye Baby" to him. She kissed the telltale smooth space between his nose and mouth, feeling fiercely protective. "Don't worry, little one. We gotcha," she whispered. He seemed wise beyond his years, beyond them all, gazing back at her with those small, dark eyes.

She reminisced about how it had been with Shawna. It was a slower reckoning with her, a creeping awareness that all wasn't as it should be. Shawna, at first just a little behind on the baby development charts, Karen feeling she failed, that somehow, if she was a better mother, her child would have acceptable scores. When Shawna reached school age, the disability was undeniable. Then, came acceptance, for the most part. But never fully, not really. She wouldn't want another mother to go through that pain, and yet... Oh, she was just exhausted. She put the baby in his porta-crib and closed her eyes.

#

At 5:30 a.m., Karen arrived at the Airbnb, with the baby in Shawna's old infant car seat. He was newly bathed, and dressed in the least girly of Shawna's old newborn sleepers, a plain yellow one. It hung off him.

Jack looked worn out, after being up all night. When she suggested he go to bed and let her take it from there, he didn't argue.

She took a Coke from the fridge, in lieu of coffee. Then she settled in with the baby on the couch after turning the TV on, hoping it would wake Shawna. She wanted to get this over with.

Shawna didn't wake up. After nearly an hour, Karen had had enough of waiting. It was excruciating to sit there and think about the life-changing trick she was about to pull on her own child. But she didn't see a better way out of it.

Karen's mind kept cycling through the situation and kept coming up with the same conclusion. Karen was in this deep now, too. She might also go to jail. And Lonnie was only a roommate. She wouldn't stick around to look out for Shawna indefinitely. And Shawna was nowhere near ready for independent living. She was very vulnerable. She might even end up like the poor girl by the highway. There was no alternative.

Karen couldn't take the waiting for one more minute. The situation needed to progress. She took the baby into the room Shawna was sleeping in.

"Shawna? Shawnie?"

Shawna opened her eyes for a second, murmured something.

Karen nudged her. "Wake up, my only Sun-Shawn. I have something for you."

Shawna sat up and rubbed her eyes. She said, "A baby?"

"That's right, honey. Your baby."

"Huh?"

"Don't you remember last night? You passed out."

"And then I had a baby?"

"You sure did. You were pregnant after all. You were right all along."

The Reunion

September brought a chill to the air but it was cozy in the apartment. Afternoon sunlight streamed through the picture window, bathing the living room in golden light. TJ's dad stirred a fragrant pot of chili on the stove. TJ lit a jar candle to complete the homey mood, imagining it as a roaring fireplace.

After baby Tony was down for his nap, she settled in at the kitchen table to make a necklace someone had ordered, crystal beads with a fancy silver clasp. The faceted beads gave off tiny rainbow arcs in the light. It was gorgeous, magical. She was trying to decide if she should make another one for herself, when there was a knock at the door.

She got up and looked through the peephole.

It was her mom.

All the way from Arizona. That was 1,600 miles away. 2,700 kilometers. Without calling first. Her heart thumped. Something must be very wrong. She yanked the door open.

"Hello, TJ," her mom said, brushing past, a suitcase in each hand.

"Oh my god. What's wrong?"

"What do you mean, 'What's wrong?' Your father can drop in on you, but I can't?" There it was again, that same bristliness about TJ's dad that her mom had shown the last time TJ spoke with her, which was weeks ago.

TJ said, "Of course you can drop in on me. You just did. Wait. What I mean is, I'm super glad you're here." She doubted anyone liked people showing up at their doorstep with their suitcases. But there were likely bigger problems than that going on right now.

TJ's mom was an odd duck, that's what she was. TJ felt disconnected from her now, after being apart from her for a year and a half. Her mom set down her suitcases and stood there.

TJ hugged her. She said, "How's Oodle?" Oodle, her mom's poodle, was one of her favorite topics of conversation.

Before her mom could answer, her dad came up behind them. He said, "Stella?"

Her mom opened her eyes comically wide, like he'd just uttered something startlingly stupid. TJ half expect her mom to reply with a childish "That's my name, don't wear it out." It wasn't very nice.

Then again, the mess her dad had made of their family was far worse than just "not very nice." Her mom hadn't had several months to resolve all that with him like TJ had.

TJ said, "Come sit down. Dad's making chili. Would you like a Coke? Or a beer? Let me take your sweater.

And your suitcases." TJ stopped chattering then. It felt weird to play hostess to her own mother. She didn't know where to put the suitcases.

Her mom said she'd have a Coke.

Her dad said, "Give her my room."

Baby Tony started crying from his crib in TJ's bedroom. So much for his nap.

A few minutes later, her mom's suitcases were in her dad's bedroom and baby Tony was in her mom's lap, smiling away at her in his most charming manner, though he'd for sure be cranky later.

They sat in the living room with glasses of Coke on ice. TJ was waiting to hear what in the world was going on but her mom's focus was on meeting her grandson. At first, TJ was proud and pleased. Then, a wave of envy washed over her. She wasn't sure if she was jealous of the attention her mom was paying to baby Tony or the attention baby Tony was paying to her mom. Now her mom's competitiveness with her dad made more sense to her, at least.

Half an hour later, they sat down at the kitchen table for an early dinner of chili, soda crackers and a quickly tossed together fruit salad. Baby Tony was in his highchair, her mom on one side of him and TJ on the other. They both tried to tend to him. TJ noticed that her jewelry components were still on the table and swept them back into their tackle box. She said, "So, how was your flight?"

"Oh, I didn't fly. Eli Falcon and his wife invited me to ride with them. He's from around here, you know."

Of course TJ knew that, since Eli Falcon was her soon-to-be ex's cousin, who her soon-to-be ex had lived with when TJ had first met him. TJ just said, "Hmm." She tried to decide how offended she should be that her mom had buddied up with Oliver's relatives, considering that Oliver blew up her life. Eli and his wife must be downstairs at Oliver's now. They were probably talking about TJ.

Eli's wife, Rose, was kind of nice but kind of bossy, in the way people tended to be when they were a decade older than you. Oliver told her once that when he'd told them TJ was pregnant, Rose started crying, then apologized all over herself for crying. Apparently, she'd been trying for a baby for years. TJ would have guessed she'd cried because TJ would finally know more about something than Rose did, so Rose wouldn't be able to give TJ a bunch of unsolicited advice about it. Rose did anyway though, until they'd moved away from Tucson. TJ would still kind of want to see Rose while she was there though, if it wasn't for Oliver.

TJ had practically developed a phobia about Oliver. She had nightmares about him taking baby Tony away. Her best hope with Oliver was just for him to continue ignoring her and baby Tony. And here was her own mother, getting all chummy with Oliver's family behind her back. TJ had figured out how offended she should be. She was very frigging offended.

Her mom and dad started catching up on old times, tersely at first. As the meal progressed, they warmed up to each other and TJ began to feel like a third wheel. Her parents had both followed her to a whole different country, uninvited, then treated *her* like the third wheel. Nice.

Everything was different now. After she and baby Tony finished eating, she cleaned him up and took him to her bedroom to play. She kept the door cracked but she didn't hear much that was of interest.

When she finally snuck a peek, her mom's face was in her hands. Her dad kneeled down in front of her.

He pulled a card out of his wallet. He said, "See dat? Now, even if anyone did bother coming to a whole nudder country just to look for old Anthony Torelli, dey wouldn't find him. He don't exist no more. Look here. Me llamo Antonio Garcia." He'd never told TJ he'd changed his name.

This visit was all starting to make sense. Her mom was still worried about that life insurance money she'd collected when Dad supposedly died. TJ's mom was most likely desperate to discuss it with her dad, and wanting as little record of being here as possible. She must have gotten a passport and used it to cross the border, though. If so, there would be a record of it. TJ waved her thoughts away. She was just guessing anyway.

She heard her dad say, "I never stopped loving you." It sounded like her mom said, "Me too."

TJ called Greta, then grabbed baby Tony and his diaper bag and went down the hall to Greta's place. Around her other, not so positive feelings about her parents right then, a warm glow seeped into her consciousness, about the possibility of them being together again. She thought maybe just about every child, of any age, wanted their parents back together again.

The warm glow wasn't without those cold spots, though. Memories of how they used to fight, though they both seem like different, more grown up, people now. And her mom's boyfriend, Bruce. He was a very decent person and if her parents got back together, TJ figured he'd be badly hurt. She guessed love was just more complicated when you were older. It would be more complicated for her too, since she had baby Tony now.

She'd never loved Oliver. She fantasized about Montie, the chick who'd kicked her out for fighting with Shawna. Shawna's surprise announcement at the mother's circle had set TJ's already turbulent feelings on fire. That's how she thought of it now, anyway.

She was barely through Greta's door when Greta said, "Sit down, girl. You're not gonna believe this shit."

TJ was still in a mixed state from her parents' unexpected reunion. She wasn't up for any more unbelievable shit. She said, "Do you have any booze?"

"Is beer okay?"

"Wonderful. Where's Emma?"

"Max has her today."

"Oh. Man. I thought you two were rock solid. We all did."

Greta shrugged. "Yeah, it sucks. But what can ya do."

"Yep, what can ya do." She settled Tony on his blanket, spread out on the living room carpet.

Greta's black kitten was barely a kitten anymore. It came over to investigate baby Tony, who wiggled and cooed, overjoyed. The cat seemed much more sanitary than it had the night Greta brought it home but TJ still didn't trust it. She sat down on the floor between it and Tony. "What's the kitty's name again?"

"Blackie."

"Oh. How original."

"Emma named her. Anyway, brace yourself, girl. I've got to tell you something and I don't think you're going to like it."

Goddamn Greta seemed about to fall out of her chair, in her eagerness to tell TJ something TJ wouldn't like. TJ took a swig of beer, then shook her head to clear out the confusion going on at home. "Okay. What is it?"

"Are you sure you're going to be okay?"

"Greta."

"Okay, okay. So, you know how Karen, Jack and Shawna went away, for like a month?"

"Yeah. On a long driving trip. And oh my god, they left Oliver in charge. I wouldn't leave Oliver in charge of a hamster."

"I think he actually did pretty well."

TJ glared at Greta until she amended her comment. "I mean, not to compliment him or anything. I mean, obviously, he's still a shithead."

"That's better. Continue, please."

Tony grabbed the cat by its ear and yelped deliriously. "Tony, no! Be nice," TJ said, prying his tiny fingers off the poor creature, one by one.

The cat ran away. Good.

"Well. They, the Shays, came home today."

"Yeah, I saw their car pull in."

"Do you already know?"

"Greta."

"Okay, okay. Well, Jiminy Christmas. While they were gone, Shawna gave birth to a baby."

"What the hell? I thought Karen said Shawna wasn't pregnant."

"She did. All I can think of is maybe she wanted Shawna to adopt it out and thought it would be better if people didn't know. That's just a guess. But you know, sometimes you can't tell with heavier people. When I was in high school, this one big girl, she had bad stomach pains and her mom took her to the emergency room and---"

"Greta." She finished her beer in three long swigs.

"Easy there, sweetie."

TJ was about to ask for another beer in spite of Greta's admonition but the mother rules that had taken over her life prevented it. She said, "Have you, um, seen this baby? Is it Native?"

"Uh, yes. The baby definitely looks Native. Well, I didn't actually see him but Max did. Max and Oliver have gotten tight since we split, you know. In fact, Max is staying at Oliver's."

"Yeah, I know." There weren't many secrets around this place. Not for long, anyway. TJ pictured Oliver with Eli, Rose and Max. All of them getting nosey. She didn't want them focusing their attention on her baby.

"So, Max just told me this when he came to get Emma a while ago. Max was hanging out in the convenience store talking to Oliver, who was working, see. Shawna's parents were in the parking lot, unpacking the car from their trip. Then, Shawna comes in holding this Native baby and says, "This is my son. My Mom said to tell you he's not yours."

"What the hell?"

Greta said, "Yeah. I know. I mean, doesn't that sound rehearsed or something? Like Shawna was sent in to the store especially to say that?"

"Yeah, it sounds strange." She was sorry she'd made that comment about not trusting Oliver with a hamster. It would probably get back to Oliver at top speed. Anything could upset the current, best possible situation, where Oliver just stayed away. TJ deliberately sighed, like it all bored her. "Eh, whatever. I'm over Oliver."

"Oh. Well, that's good. I mean, it doesn't bother you if Oliver and Shawna were getting together, behind your back?" Greta peered at her intently.

"Nah. Aw, look at Tony. Out like a light. Aren't they sweet when they're asleep?"

"Yeah, they're dolls when they're asleep. So, I guess this means Oliver will have to split his time and money between two kids and two baby mamas now."

"Eh. Whatever." She didn't tell Greta that Oliver hadn't seen Tony in weeks, or that she didn't plan to ask for child support. The last thing she needed was Greta stirring things up.

Greta could just sit there and get excited about her own divorce. She'd had enough of Greta. She said, "So, I just wanted to stop by and say hey. Thanks for the beer."

"What, you're leaving already?"

"Yep. Gotta go."

"Oh. Well, call me any time if you want to talk, sweetie. It seems we're in the same boat nowadays."

Greta liked to talk about what was in everybody else's boat and keep her own business to herself. TJ mumbled a good-bye and somehow shut the door behind her, loaded down as she was with a still sleeping Tony and the giant diaper bag.

She didn't know who else's kid Shawna's son could be besides Oliver's, if he looked Native. Come to think of it, maybe Shawna had done her a favor. Oliver having to deal with that baby made it less likely he'd have time to come after her baby. The stupid fight she got into with Shawna seemed like it was years ago.

Now what? She didn't want to interrupt her parents' reunion. Their reconnection seemed so new and fragile that any tiny interruption might break it.

She was right next to Lonnie's apartment. She knocked on the door, momentarily, stupidly, forgetting that Shawna might be home. She'd gotten used to Shawna being out of town. Oh well, they'd have to see each other sometime. She tried to think of what to say right then that didn't sound totally pushy and Greta-like, such as "Can I come in?" Lonnie cracked the door open. She just kind of stood there with a question on her face. TJ said, "Can you come out and play?"

It broke the ice. Lonnie said, "Get in here, ya mooncalf."

Lonnie said, "Want some coffee? I just made a pot."

"Sure." She lay Tony and his blanket on the carpet. "I was just passing by and decided to bother you."

"I'm flattered. So, whatcha been up to?"

"Not much. Taking care of Tony. Working on my jewelry business. You know, the usual. How about you? Do you still have that job, helping that old couple?"

"Yep. They're great. I get four days off a week, since I stay at their place for three days straight. Well, the four days off might be ending soon, seeing as how I've lost my roommate."

"Shawna moved out?"

"Yep. Karen and Jack are giving me two months before I have to start paying the full rent. You heard Shawna surprised us all with a baby, didn't you?"

"I did." Here it was again.

"Yeah. I don't think Karen trusts Shawna with the baby on her own. I'd be happy to help out some. But then, I'm gone half the week, for one thing."

"Sure. That makes sense."

There was a long silence. TJ didn't want to say anything interesting enough to find its way back to Oliver.

Lonnie brought two cups of coffee. She said, "I've got real sugar, fake sugar and milk."

"Fake sugar, please. Hey, Greta might be looking for a roommate."

Lonnie kind of laughed, which TJ didn't understand. Greta could be super irritating but living with her was better than being homeless.

Max walked in. He didn't knock. He just walked right in. "Hey, baby," he said to Lonnie, before he noticed TJ.

Max froze in place. Lonnie shrugged, like *well, I guess we're busted.* She said, "You're early."

So, Max and Lonnie had a thing going on. TJ couldn't take any more drama today. She said, "I better get going."

Lonnie said, "Stay and drink your coffee."

So she did but only because running out the door without finishing the coffee seemed rude.

Lonnie said, "Please don't say anything, all right? Not that we're doing anything wrong because we're not. Greta and Max are over and Greta's the one who ended it. And there was absolutely nothing going on between us, before that."

"Of course. And listen, you don't have to explain anything to me anyway."

Max sat next to Lonnie, and leaned over to give her a long, French kiss. TJ noticed that Lonnie's head was quite a bit larger than Max's.

They both looked up suddenly, like they'd been startled. Like TJ shouldn't have been watching, or shouldn't even be there, when she'd just been told to stay. When they were the ones putting on the show in front of her. Remembering that Max was staying with Oliver, TJ said, "Okay, let's make a deal. I won't say anything about you two, and you two don't give Oliver any information about me. Nothing at all, ever. Like, not even that I was here."

"You got it," Max said.

"Sure," Lonnie said.

Max stared into his shirt pocket and Lonnie patted the pocket, like it was her imaginary friend in there, too. They made scrunchy baby faces at each other. TJ downed the rest of her coffee and left.

Back at the apartment, TJ's parents were in her dad's bedroom with the door closed. She heard the bedsprings creak, which was super gross. She had to get out of there again, right away.

But to where? Oliver's pals hung out in the basement. She'd already been to Greta's, and to Lonnie's. Shawna was at Karen's, so she couldn't go there. And Oliver's apartment was the last place on earth she'd want to go. There was only one place left, Wayne the trucker's apartment. She didn't know him that well but he seemed like a nice old guy. He reminded her of her mom's boyfriend, Bruce. Poor Bruce. Anyway, old people liked company, didn't they?

Nobody answered Wayne's door. She knocked again. Still no answer. She didn't know what got into her then, she really didn't, but on an impulse, she tried to turn the doorknob. It was locked.

She thought to check under the doormat. And there was a key, like it was just waiting for her. Like an invitation. She unlocked the door and went inside.

She'd heard Wayne was an artist, when he wasn't busy being a truck driver, but she didn't expect what she saw. There was a lot of art. Real art, like signed original oil paintings. She felt as if she'd stepped through a portal into a magical world, like she'd read about in some children's book years ago.

In the corner stood a life-sized statue of some kind of young warrior, carved out of stone. It looked to her like it belonged in a museum.

The main thing, though, were the rainbows. Dozens of small rainbow fragments floated through the living room.

The big picture window was entirely covered in a web of faceted crystal prisms with holes in them, like TJ's crystal jewelry beads, but larger. They were connected by what looked like the same thing she strung hers with for jewelry, clear fishing line.

Baby Tony stared, transfixed. They were swimming in tiny floor to ceiling rainbows. She'd never seen anything like it. It was drop-dead gorgeous. Other-worldly, even.

A car honked outside. What the hell was she doing?

She rushed to the door and looked through the peephole. No one was in sight, so she stepped out with baby Tony, stuck the key under the mat and ran back up the stairs to her dad's place. Once inside, she locked the door. She leaned against it, trying to catch her breath.

It was quiet in her dad's apartment now. She guessed old people didn't do it for very long. That cracked her up, in a slimy way. She carried Tony to the kitchen, looking for a snack, trying to figure out what had just frigging happened.

All she could think of was that she'd acted crazy after a crazy day. And maybe she was tired of always accepting whatever was dropped on her. Maybe she wanted to try being a wild thing for a change, like Oliver. Or a criminal, like her parents, she thought, trying out that label in her mind.

She grabbed a handful of animal crackers, gave a couple to Tony (a giraffe and a bear) and ate a couple herself, being sure to bite their heads off first. She had a lion and a zebra or donkey, she couldn't tell for sure. She strutted around the living room in circles, with Tony on her hip, feeling bad-ass. She imagined Montie admiring her, Montie maybe even confessing that the fight TJ had with Shawna had actually, secretly, turned Montie on. She felt like maybe she hadn't been herself for most of her life. Maybe she was somebody, after all.

Art Within Art

Wayne returned from his over-the-road haul to find a baby's pacifier inside his apartment, on the floor by the front door. He turned it in his hand, trying to figure out how the heck it could have gotten there.

His best guess would have been that a baby in its parent's arms happened to drop its pacifier into one of the plastic bags on the bag holder rack at Walmart, then Wayne's groceries had been placed in that bag. But then it would have had to undergo a second mishap too, falling out of the bag after he got home. And then, he'd also have had to not notice it, in the two days between his grocery shopping trip and going to work.

That was a bit of a long shot in itself but no, come to think of it, Walmart stopped offering plastic bags a while back. Now you had to bring your own. Taking away the free plastic bags was the talk of Nomads Nest for a time. Karen was all for less single-use plastic but Greta was hopping mad, since then she had to pay for rolls of small plastic bags for her cat's daily litterbox scooping. Yep, pretty radical debates around here. Now, you could purchase tote bags at the checkout counter and he supposed a baby could have dropped its pacifier into one of those. But nope, he'd remembered to bring his own tote bags for a change, last time.

The dull ache in his head had progressed to a killer headache. He got a lot of headaches these days. Maybe he should drink more water. Or retire and have less stress. Or… something. He'd already gone to the doctor, after Sarah kept nagging him to. That got him a prescription for some pills that would basically knock him out when the headaches got too bad. Of course, he'd rather if they'd found a cause and a cure for his headaches. But he was very grateful for the meds when he needed them. Those little rainbows sprinkled all over the living room from his latest phase, his prism art, they made him want to vomit. They were so bright and sparkly that he couldn't stand looking at them, with his headache. He needed his meds with a big glass of water, and then a nice nap.

#

When he awoke, it was nearly evening and the living room rainbows had calmed down, thank god. He disassembled the network of crystals in the picture window. Then he disassembled the glass rectangles filled with colored waters, left over from his art interest before the prisms. It was all very off-putting to him now. But then, this was how it always went, with his phases.

Art, to him, was like a fling with a sexy but unbalanced woman. He'd fall hard for a concept or medium or what-have-you and be totally obsessed with it for a while. Then, one day, the limerence period would be over, the magic would be gone.

Then, he couldn't move on from it fast enough. The bold, flashy colors of the colored waters looked garish now, in front of the dull grey parking lot outside and the dry, chilly prairie beyond. It was all wrong, stale and mildly sickening, like having Christmas lights still up in September. And that's even aside from the headache that made bright colors and sparkly things intolerable.

A new art phase had been on his mind, though. He headed down to his truck to get the microscope he'd bought on this last trip. Outside his door, he almost bumped into Shawna, who was carrying a baby. Karen was right behind her, scolding her about something or other. Karen said, "Shawna! Say hello to Mr. Wayne."

"Hello," Shawna said, sulky.

"Hi. Whose kid?"

Shawna said, "Mine." Her usual big smile appeared.

Karen said, "Yes. Hers." She rolled her eyes, in put-upon mother fashion.

"Oh. Well. Congratulations! What's his name?"

"Nicholas."

"Cool. Hey, are you missing a pacifier, by any chance? I found one. Hold on…" He stepped back into his apartment and grabbed it. "Is this yours?"

"No," Shawna and Karen said, in unison.

Karen said, "Nicholas uses newborn pacifiers. That one's for an older baby."

"Oh, right. I forgot. It's been a long time since I had a baby around. You ladies have a nice evening, now." So,

Shawna had a baby. Geez. Poor Karen. The kid looked Native, just like Oliver. That boy needed some direction in life, before somebody shot him.

He proceeded down the stairs and out to the parking lot, wishing he'd grabbed his jacket. His old bones didn't tolerate the cold like they used to. He found the bag with the microscope in it and took it back upstairs. He got it at a truck stop, of all places. He'd bought it because it went with an idea that had been forming in his mind. You never knew what you'd find at a truck stop. It was a kids' microscope but it would do.

Back inside, he set an upside-down drinking glass on top of a piece of computer paper and traced around it, then moved the glass and traced around it again, until he had a few circles drawn on the paper.

Then he put some dish soap on a slide, looked at it under the microscope, and sketched what he saw, in one of the little circles. He labeled it "Dish Soap." He'd do these rough sketches, then decide which ones were interesting enough to paint later. One at a time, he put things on the slide: bread crumbs, a fingernail clipping, spit. He vaguely recalled having to look at various things under a microscope like this in science class back in his school days. A lot of his art inspirations came from childhood memories.

Later, when he was done for the time being, he grabbed a beer and sat down to relax in front of the television. He spotted a single long brown hair on his coffee table, curled like an infinity symbol. He put it under the microscope and sketched it.

No women had been in Wayne's place since... probably since Sarah had brought her car by for him to work on. That was at least three weeks ago. Her hair was short though, and bleached blonde, or maybe it was grey now. It was hard to tell. And he was a bit of a neat freak; he kept his place clean. A lone, long hair on his coffee table didn't make sense.

He remembered the pacifier. Someone had been in here while he was gone. After sketching the hair under the microscope, he sealed it into a sandwich bag along with the pacifier and stuck it in his kitchen junk drawer. The only girl here with a baby, besides Shawna now, was TJ. She had long brown hair. Shawna's was white-blonde. If he got a chance, he'd get hold of one of her hairs and compare it to the one he already had. He looked around his apartment but nothing seemed to be missing. Even the stack of cash in his top dresser drawer was still there, undisturbed.

He remembered the key under his doormat, and retrieved it. He'd told Oliver it was there a few months back, told him to pass the message on to Lonnie, in case she needed somewhere to stay. She had long brown hair too, but no baby, as far as he knew. Babies seemed to be showing up overnight now, though, so who knew.

Remembering when he worried about Lonnie having a safe place to sleep made him think of Sarah and Fleura-Dania. What if they ever needed a refuge and he wasn't around? Geez, if somebody here needed a place to go, all they'd have to do was ask him. What did he care, anyhow? He opened the door and put the key back under the mat.

#

A few days later, he'd just finished eating a plate of microwaved potatoes, topped with shredded cheddar, onion and chopped tomatoes, when TJ came to visit. It seemed strange, when he didn't know her that well. Especially after… He said, "TJ. What's up?"

"Hi there. Just thought I'd stop by and bother you. That is, if you're not busy or anything. I mean, it's just fine if you are. I just---"

"Sure. Come on in, darlin'. Golly, that boy's getting big. Have a seat. You want a Dr. Pepper?"

"Yeah, that'd be great. Thanks." She spread her baby's blanket out on the carpet and put the kid on it, then grabbed a couple of bright plastic toys from a diaper bag. He considered handing her the pacifier to see what she did. He decided not to.

"So, whatcha know, kid?" he said, handing her a glass of soda on ice. The obvious conversation starter now would be Shawna's baby. That was the big news here. He caught himself, remembering who the baby's father might be.

She said, "Oh, not much. I've been going around the building, visiting a lot this week. My mom's here from Arizona. It's a small place for four of us.

"Ah, gotcha." Breaking into his place just to get some peace and quiet seemed pretty extreme to him but then young people were prone to extremes sometimes. He hadn't recalled the girl being this young. He wondered if she was even out of her teens. "Well listen kid, if my car or my rig are gone, I'm gone, so feel free to come on in, any time it gets too cramped over there."

Her eyes widened, then she seemed to regain her composure. She said, "Oh, wow. Thanks. That's really, super generous."

"No problem, darlin'. The key's under the doormat."

"Where's your prisms and stuff?" she said, then her eyes definitely widened. Of course, she shouldn't know that he had "prisms and stuff." She said, "Uh, I mean. I heard you had done something really cool with prisms or something like that."

He felt a little sorry for her. She looked so rattled. And she had Oliver's kid. The poor thing. He said, "I'm on to a new phase now, just starting it. It's not as flashy, though. You know, to me, art is like playing, like when you're a little kid and you'd just lose yourself in whatever you were playing at." Here he went, talking about art to a non-artist, setting himself up to be annoyed. He couldn't think of anything else to say to her, though.

He continued rambling on. "I got the inspiration for the prisms one winter day when I was outdoors and an ice-covered tree caught my eye. The sun shining on the ice that coated the little branches created zillions of tiny rainbow fragments. I was blown away. Never forgot it. Missed my haircut appointment completely because I couldn't tear myself away from looking at that amazing tree of rainbows. Nature's chandelier. Anyway…"

He brought his pile of sketches and paintings over. "See, now I'm doing paintings from what I see under a microscope, but larger and more colorful. People not knowing what the design represents adds an extra layer of something, I think. It would look like a random design to other people but it might have deeper meaning to you, in some way."

"Cool. Like in what way do you mean?"

"Eh, I don't know. Say the design is from a slide of… somebody's wedding cake or… their baby's hair or a zillion other things."

"That's really different," she said. She looked through his artwork. "That's really different. Super cool! This one is so intricate. I keep thinking I might see hidden images in these. Like that right there. Did you mean to hide a little lion head in there? No? Hmm."

Finally, she said, "I make jewelry and sell it online. I get lots of special orders. I bet you'd make a mint doing personalized microscope paintings for people."

Would wonders never cease. A non-stupid idea that came from talking about his art to a non-artist. Then again, she might be an artist, if she made jewelry. He said, "You know, that's not a bad idea. Not half bad. I'm about ready to retire anyway. A shoestring business would be just right, something to transition into."

After a while, TJ said she had to go. She said, "I'll be happy to help you set up an online shop. Any time. Just let me know."

"Thanks. I'll probably take you up on that. And I meant it, about the key under the doormat. If you want to get away and the place is empty, you just come on in."

She left. He wondered if he'd been idiotically generous. After all, he really didn't know the kid and she had probably actually committed a crime against him that she could have gotten jail time for. Just because she didn't steal anything that time didn't mean she didn't intend to.

Eh, hell with it. If her coming in got to be a problem, he'd just change the lock.

He worked on his microscope art some more. He painted the microscopic image of a drop of beer, large and colorized. He tried to think of what type of special orders he could show on a sales page. He'd have to make a note prohibiting people from sending him any gross bodily fluids.

He got engrossed in his microscope paintings until a nasty headache overcame him. He'd drank plenty of water so maybe it was allergies or the smoke blowing in from a wildfire. He took his headache meds with a glass of water. They kicked in quick and then he felt good enough to clean up from painting, wash up his dishes, straighten his place before bed. He was feeling high enough from the dose of meds that he forgot he'd already taken it. He was feeling fine and wanted to feel finer. He took his meds all over again. As soon as his head hit the pillow, he was out.

The smoke alarm woke him up. That, and the smell of burning.

The Tulpa Transfer

Everyone else was going on and on about how terrible the fire was. But after being sure she was going to be snuffed out in it, Min just felt blessed.

She got tired of human whining anyway. As someone who didn't even possess her own body, well, they'd have to pardon her ass if she didn't have a ton of sympathy about somebody's couch or Coach purse being ruined by the smoke. (From what they were all saying, you could never get the smoke odor out of soft goods. You'd have to throw them away).

Min had smelled the smoke and heard the alarms and everyone else rushing out of the building. But she couldn't do a thing but wait, paralyzed, for the fire to come burn them up. Her idiot bodylord, Max, had been too wasted to wake up.

She and Max were staying in the basement, because Oliver's cousins were visiting from Tucson and Oliver's place only had one bedroom. So Min and Max had to sleep in the basement truckers' quarters, hidden away. They weren't really supposed to be there.

Thank god Oliver thought of them. He came charging down the basement stairs, yelling, as the place filled with smoke. He dragged drunk, dumbass Max to his feet and frog marched him up the stairs and out the door, Min riding along in Max's shirt pocket. Oh, cool night air never felt so heavenly. She hoped Wayne would paint it, the building in flames with the black night around it. She pictured giant stars, swirling above it all. She'd title such a painting "Midnight Mint." That was the part that stuck in her mind now, not the smoke or the fire but the mint fresh air, once they got outside. Of course, she'd never have made it this far if she wasn't an extreme optimist.

That Oliver, though. Even as he was wrestling Max up the steps, he'd remembered her. He said, "Hey, Min. Doing all right, dear?" Man, she loved that guy.

Max, in contrast, insulted Oliver, as Oliver was saving their lives. He slurred, "Ooh woo, here's the great Native sage. All in touch with that which cannot be seen. Ooh woo."

Stupid Max was the one who thought he was some great mystic, just because he had her, Min. He got jealous whenever he remembered that Oliver perceived her existence, too. Greta couldn't perceive Min. She was simply too thickly earthbound to have the ability. She didn't want to know Min, anyway. She wanted to exterminate Min.

Lonnie couldn't perceive Min either but she acted like she could, trying to impress Max. Min found it hilarious. She had no idea how much he hated it when she tried to join in on the tulpa thing. Max wanted Lonnie to think of him as special and unique, not to tell him that she could do everything he could do.

Oliver didn't give a shit what Max thought, whether Max was drunk or sober. In response to Max's insults, he replied, bored, "It is what it is. There now, watch your step, dude."

The residents of Nomads Nest were gathered in the grass beyond the parking lot now, watching the firefighters knock back the blaze.

Karen said to her husband Jack, "Dammit, I knew this would happen. I knew it! Those damn sparks along the train tracks. Didn't I tell you?"

"You did, babe. You sure did." They were sitting on his jacket, his arm around her. She was rocking the baby, as much as she could while seated on the ground. Shawna slept on the grass next to her parents. Her jacket was balled up into a makeshift pillow and she was snoring. Shawna probably didn't care about the fire. It would all be her parents' problem.

Oliver stayed on the far edge of the gathering, with his cousin Eli and Eli's wife, Rose. Oliver kept a low profile because some of the women didn't like him.

A fluttering spirit caught Min's attention. The spirit hovered around Karen and the baby, Nicholas. It was that Nila girl again, the one who was found dead by the highway a couple of months back.

Min wondered, not for the first time, what that was all about. Spirits and tulpas differed from each other but shared similarities, too. The differences between them were along the same lines as, oh, horses versus zebras. Or lions versus tigers. Llamas versus alpacas. Something like that. The spirits Min saw were usually recently split from their bodies, newly deceased. They generally hung around the people (or pets) who were closest to their hearts. They only stuck around for a little while, though. Once they felt reassured that their cherished one was all right, they'd move on. Min wondered if perhaps Nila had lost her way somehow, gotten confused and ended up with the wrong family.

But Min had other things on her mind right then. She observed the gathered people closely. She'd been thinking about leaving Max for a while now. But a gal like her needed a host in order to survive, and her host must be able to perceive her.

There weren't a whole lot of people like that around. They'd usually be people who didn't fit with the mainstream. Your creative types, some religious types. Some mentally ill people, marginalized people, lonely people. These were the types most likely to be able to create tulpas, or able to perceive and accept tulpas who already existed. She didn't think Max especially fit the profile. Yet, he'd created her. You just never knew.

Min would love to go with Oliver and had even discussed it with him once, when Max was passed out. But Oliver said having a tulpa, even Min, just wasn't for him. It would be a life complication, and he said he'd realized that wasn't something he was good at.

Goddamn Greta came thundering over, with her kid on her hip. She was mad about something or other, as usual. She was always trying to make people think Max was some big drunk now, which he was. However, he'd hardly drank at all when he was with her. He drank because she broke his heart.

Greta set the kid down, rolled Max over and started rifling through his pants pockets. She pulled the cash out of his wallet and stuck it into her bra. Then she returned his empty wallet to his pocket and rolled him back into place once more. She picked up the kid and stomped off the way she'd come. Max slept through it all. Oliver and his cousin laughed their asses off. The cousin's wife shook her head.

A man from Jack and Karen Shay's insurance company drove up. He consulted with the couple. Then the rest of us were told that the insurance policy belonged to Jack and Karen but somehow the rest of us still qualified for temporary lodging in a large house the insurance representative had arranged for all of us to stay in. For anything more than that, we'd have to consult our individual renters' policies, if we had them.

So, the residents of all six apartments piled into assorted vehicles and headed out in a row, to a large old farmhouse in Fireweed City. Max, Min, Oliver and Oliver's cousins were to ride with Wayne, who was helping Oliver jostle Max to Wayne's car. Max (and Min) got in the passenger seat, next to Wayne.

As they travelled down the road, in a line with the other cars, Min felt it. Wayne glanced over at her a couple of times, though he was driving, and of course nobody could really see her. Rather, he *perceived* her. And she perceived that he perceived her.

Min was too interconnected with Max to be able to hate him. It was more that Min didn't trust Max to care for her anymore. He was too much of a mess himself to be a good bodylord. For example, he'd just nearly gotten both of them killed.

Wayne said he felt one of his headaches coming, when they were nearly to the farmhouse. He asked Max to grab his meds out of the glove box. Max did. When Max handed the bottle of pills to Wayne, Min was ready. She took her chance, hopping from Max's hand to Wayne's hand. From there, she climbed up Wayne's arm, toward his shirt pocket. She was so nervous that she feared she'd pass out. Wayne stiffened for a second. He perceived her. She flipped into his pocket and lay inside it, panting. The transfer was complete.

At the Farmhouse

The fire was a lucky break for Greta, though of course it would sound terrible to say so. It gave her a while longer to figure out her next move. She certainly didn't miss being in competition with a delusion, for her husband's affections. It had become intolerable. The Other Woman, imaginary as she was, was clearly the one Max wanted more and she could have him. But being a single mother with no job skills wasn't working out any better for, so far. In fact, it was starting to seem like it was going to be even worse.

She'd worked it out on paper, several times. Even if she got a job and a roommate, she still wouldn't be able to make it, not very well anyway. She could probably find work somewhere like a restaurant, laundromat or convenience store, here in Fireweed City or over in Morton. But the estimated child support payments would barely cover the cost of a babysitter. She'd also need to keep up her car, to be able to get to whatever lousy job she was able to find.

She wished she was an accountant. Then she'd be able to work from home, like Max did. She'd have it made. She could have gotten an accounting degree online these past few years. But she'd stayed at home and complained about being bored instead, dammit. It just wasn't where her mind was at, at the time. She didn't know where her damn mind had been at the time.

It had been a crazy week. First, there was the fire. And now they had six apartments worth of people crammed into a six-bedroom house. There were fourteen people here at the farmhouse, divided into bedrooms as follows:

1-Greta and little Emma

2-Wayne, Max and Oliver. (Oliver's cousins went somewhere else, after seeing that there just wasn't any extra room for guests).

3- TJ and baby Tony

4- Tony Senior and Stella

5- Jack and Karen Shay

6- Shawna Shay, baby Nicholas and Lonnie

That was fourteen people, including the babies, all sharing one kitchen, two bathrooms and one washer/dryer combo. Thankfully, at some point in the past, someone added that second bathroom and the laundry room onto this old house. Greta had been afraid they'd have to use an outhouse and wash clothes by hand, like Hutterites.

Karen had them organized like a boardinghouse, which caused some grumbling but probably kept the place from being a complete madhouse. They had assigned bath times, assigned chores and assigned laundry days, written out on a chart that hung on the wall. Meals were eaten communally, at three pushed-together dining tables: breakfast, lunch and dinner at set times, with a list of available snacks taped to the refrigerator door. (Currently, it was apples, soda crackers and nut butter).

Going into the kitchen and fixing yourself something to eat, like you could in your own place, wasn't allowed, which sucked. But the many inconveniences here were at least a little bit balanced out by a kind of party atmosphere. Aside from all the squabbles, of course.

Karen and Jack's insurance covered the basic lodging here for them all. And then donations poured in from all over this part of Alberta. The fire was big news around here. The residents slept on donated bedding, wore donated clothing and ate donated food. There was a lot of talk around the dinner table about people moving on, not wanting to live like college kids until the apartments were restored. But all fourteen of them were still here for now, plus Greta's cat. A cat was the last thing Greta needed right now but she didn't have the heart to get rid of it. Oh yeah, and there was also one fucking homewrecking tulpa-whore in residence.

It was Greta's night to cook dinner. A few people lounged around the living room, watching TV. Emma "helped" her by rinsing the salad tomatoes in a sink half full of water. Greta put a large pot of water on to boil for the donated noodles. Donated jarred spaghetti sauce heated up in another pot and green beans simmered in a third pot. Someone knocked at the door but she'd let someone else get it. She continued chopping lettuce. Shawna answered the door, carrying Nicholas with her.

It was a reporter. This was the fifth or sixth time a reporter had come by since the fire. "Reporter!" Shawna yelled in warning, thinking she was being hilarious. It had become a joke around here, how a couple of residents ran from publicity. The couple of people were Tony Sr. and Oliver. They immediately scurried upstairs whenever a reporter appeared. Greta didn't think it was funny. Neither of them seemed shy to her so what were they hiding from? She thought it proved that they were quite possibly shady. Therefore, maybe even dangerous. Subtleties like that went right over Shawna's head. It was a good thing Karen was around to watch that girl.

Shawna was out on the front porch now, talking to the reporter. Greta heard them both laughing. Karen must have heard something too because she came flying down the stairs and out to the porch. She called to Shawna, "Someone's on the phone for you, on my phone. It's in my bedroom."

Shawna came in, still holding the baby, and went upstairs to Karen's room. Shortly afterwards, Karen came back in. She entered the kitchen and rooted around in the junk drawer for a pen. She made a sign on a sheet of computer paper, *PLEASE RESPECT OUR PRIVACY!!! NO REPORTERS*!!! She stepped outside and taped it to the door. She looked frazzled. Greta said, "Is everything okay?"

"Yeah. Why?"

"Well, you look upset. And are you sure about that sign? I mean, keeping the fire in the news is what's keeping the donations rolling in, for all of us. Right?"

"Don't worry about it, goddamn Greta," Karen snarled.

"Jiminy Christmas," Greta muttered, hurt. Karen was a nice lady, usually. She didn't snarl.

Shawna came back down, telling Karen there was nobody on the phone.

Karen snapped, "Don't you be talking to any reporters, you hear me? In fact, you stay away from that goddamn door completely. From now on, you do not answer the door. At all. Got it?"

Nicholas started crying. Karen snatched him from Shawna and proceeded up the steps, her words trailing behind her. "You better damn well keep this baby out of the public eye. There are all kinds of weirdos out there, you know."

Shawna looked dazed. Her gaze met Greta's and they both kind of shrugged. Nicholas cried louder from upstairs. Shawna started crying, too.

It dawned on Greta, then. Karen was from a different generation and these small towns were old school and gossipy. Karen was embarrassed about Shawna's baby not having a father. Karen didn't want everybody to see Shawna and her illegitimate baby on the local news. It all made sense now.

Poor Shawna's crying increased to keening. She really was like a little kid sometimes. Greta said, "It's okay, Shawn-Shawn. She's just upset because of the fire and everything, sweetie. Don't worry. Hey, I saw some lemon cookies in the pantry. Let's sneak one."

That cheered Shawna up. Emma yelled, "Cookie!" Tony Sr. and Oliver, back downstairs now that the reporter had been run off, chimed in, "Cookies. We want cookies." TJ looked up from her place on the floor in front of the coffee table, where she was doing some beadwork. "Yeah, cookies," she said. The last thing Greta needed was for Karen to catch her breaking one of the rules right then, when she'd already about took Greta's head off just for trying to be helpful. "Perfect," she said, hurriedly passing out lemon cookies, shushing everyone as she went.

Max came down. The wall clock said 5:30, the end of his workday. Wayne and Oliver stayed out of the bedroom they shared with Max on weekdays, so Max could work. He said, "Can I have a cookie?"

She handed him the last two and hid the empty package under some other trash in the kitchen wastebasket.

Max said, "I need to talk to you."

"Talk away."

"No, I mean alone. When you get time."

"Okay," she said, suspicious. She stirred the pots, adjusted the heat controls and broke noodles into the boiling water. Then she straightened the big bible that she used as a booster seat for Emma, going through the dinner headcount in her mind. TJ's baby would be in the highchair. Shawna's baby didn't use a highchair yet. Wayne and Lonnie were away working and Jack was doing something over at the fire damaged truck stop. She'd need to set the table for nine.

Karen came in with a couple bottles of red. "Wine tonight," she said, plunking them down on the counter.

She patted Greta's shoulder as she passed by, a silent apology.

At dinner, Greta got a couple of compliments on the spaghetti. She felt so low on the human value scale these days that it was a nice lift, though she knew they were only being polite. It was just very basic spaghetti.

Karen reminded Oliver that it was his night to wash dishes. As Greta wiped spaghetti sauce off Emma's face, Max said, "Talk now?"

Oh god. What else could happen to her. She followed him to her bedroom, Emma in tow. "What?" she said.

He said, "I love you."

She didn't want to go through this shit again. He didn't love her enough to be normal and it had driven her to the brink. He'd ruined her life with his moronic, insane imaginary girlfriend that he absolutely refused to give up. Then he had the gall to follow her around, pleading. Begging her to stay but not bothering to make it so she could bear to.

It was pretty damn bad when she couldn't stand the thought of going back to him, even considering the bleakness of her other options, like dire poverty, for example. She lay on the bed and put the pillow over her face. Emma came along and pushed down on the pillow, squealing with laughter.

Greta said, "Thank you for the mercy killing, baby."

Max said, "Min is gone."

"Well then, you better call ghostbusters to go find her. Or the UFO committee. Or something. Dickhead."

Emma shrieked, "Dickhead!"

"Nice. Super parenting, there," Max said.

"Look who's talking."

"Wait. Let's start over here. I love you, I miss you and the tulpa is gone. The tulpa is over. Finito. Happy now?"

Her answer flew out of her mouth, before she had a chance to think about it. "Yes."

Then they had what she supposed was the expected thing, a Disney ending style kiss and hug, with little Emma joining in.

But what Greta felt was relief, not passion. A reality show she'd watched flashed through her mind, where brides and grooms from poor backward countries married less attractive but relatively much wealthier Westerners. Well, Max was attractive enough, physically. She'd thought so at one time, anyway.

He said, "Can I move in now?" As if he was afraid she'd change her mind.

She nodded and he went to his bedroom to get started, Emma scampering after him.

She felt a little guilty, then angry that she should feel at all guilty, when he was the reason they'd come to this in the first place.

He hadn't given her the full surrender that she'd been insisting on, before they broke. That would be him admitting that the tulpa had never existed, was not real. But the tulpa was gone, and that was good enough for now.

Moving On

Karen's communal breakfasts and lunches had been scrapped. They weren't practical, when people's daily schedules varied so much. But, apparently fearing that the kitchen would turn into utter Bedlam otherwise, she'd insisted anyway until everyone complained all together at the dinner table one evening. Now, sitting alone at the pushed-together tables with her coat on for warmth, Lonnie finished up her microwaved oatmeal and raisins. Neither the October morning chill nor the housework that awaited her could dull her spark today. She washed her dishes, then hurried upstairs with the broom and dustpan.

Her chore for the day was to sweep the second story. It was a lot but she jumped in, eager to get it out of the way. TJ had borrowed her dad's car and she and TJ were going to get their hair done at some chick's house on the other side of Fireweed City. The hairdresser's name was Montie. Lonnie always felt a solidarity with other chicks who had masculine sounding names. It seemed a mark against them from the start, like their parents had wanted a boy. She knew hers had.

TJ had said she was nervous about going to Montie's, because this was the girl who had kicked TJ and Shawna out of her house, after the two of them got in a fight there. From what Greta said, those two were down on the damn floor, pounding each other in front of all the nice ladies and their babies, at the mothers' circle. What a calamity. Lonnie could picture Shawna doing that, maybe, but not TJ.

Lonnie suspected TJ only invited her along because she was afraid to face this Montie chick alone. Lonnie didn't understand it, when there was a perfectly good hair salon over in Morton. If Lonnie had been kicked out of somebody's house in disgrace, she'd be too mortified to ever show up there again. TJ had even made Lonnie call to get their appointments.

But Lonnie wasn't that interested in TJ's drama. She was interested in looking extra hot for her date tonight. She had a feeling it might be a very special one. She planned to go for the balayage look with her hair, and she'd wear her shimmery red dress. She'd make Max forget all about losing his goofy tulpa. A grown man, sulking because his imaginary friend left him for someone else was just... Well, it was just her luck, really.

But nobody was perfect. And besides being kind and smart, the dude was packing. Not in length but thickness, which was what counted.

Also, she couldn't get enough of the smell of Max. Not his cologne but *him*. His sweat? She didn't know but she'd never felt that with any other guy. She'd fallen hard for him.

She hoped they'd go to Ray's Ribs. They had open mic night there on Fridays, which was as hopping as the nightlife got around here. She hoped to convince Max to move out of this podunk place. Preferably to Los Angeles. She'd lived in cold climates all her life and didn't think she could stand one more northern winter. She dreamed of palm trees and auditions and could kick herself for not heading straight to LA in the first place. But who would have been able to think straight at the time, after what she'd been put through. Besides, then she wouldn't have Max. Well, if he insisted, she'd settle for NYC. Maybe even Vancouver, if absolutely necessary. He was worth it.

But her immediate goal was to go on a date with Max tonight, and to look fabulous doing it. She'd brought up the open mic night last week but wasn't sure if his answer was yes or just maybe. He was all depressed over losing Min but getting out would help get his mind off it. If she had to, she'd even go out parking somewhere with him like they usually did lately, like teenagers. She was getting damn fed up with having to hide from Greta, though.

The tulpa issue was unique enough to fascinate her, at first. At first. She didn't say it to him but she was glad that nonsense was behind them now. She'd figured out right away that the so-called tulpa was nothing more than Max's repressed side coming out, anyway. As an accountant who worked alone from home, and as someone who'd had a very controlling wife, she got the strong impression that Max's life had been all boring and buttoned down, before he got together with her.

Lonnie daydreamed that she was in a soap opera, a humble but beautiful maid in a luxury hotel, sweeping the floors where her true love, the dashing billionaire Maximillion, resided. The narrator in her mind said, *It was obvious to all but the lovely Lancome herself that she, alone, was the reason the tulpa had departed. Now that Maximillion had her, he no longer required an alter ego to be his source of joy, his twin flame, his soul mate. Maximillion doesn't even quite realize it himself, yet. But he will. Oh yes, he will.*

No doubt, Maximillion is eager to progress with Lancome. Something may even occur tonight. And why should it wait? Lancome and Maximillion were two wounded people who had made each other whole again. And love doesn't get any truer or deeper than that, my friends.

It's not too soon for a proposal, though of course, the wedding must wait for his divorce to be final. Not to despair, the lovers shall rent a cozy cottage together in the meantime, far away from the troublesome, tiresome goddamn Greta.

Lonnie's beautiful daytime drama was interrupted by the sight of Shawna's clothes and empty snack packages, scattered across the floor. It was bad enough that Lonnie had to share a small bedroom with Shawna and her kid (though baby Nicholas *was* adorable). She wasn't picking up Shawna's mess too, not today. She pushed the mess aside with the broom without slowing down, though still annoyed that the clutter was there in the first place. Even the clothes that did somehow, miraculously make it into Shawna's laundry basket were a mess. Shawna didn't fold the clean ones before the wrinkles set in, let alone put them away. And now there were dirty clothes mixed in with the clean ones.

Lonnie had gone through it with Shawna over and over again, picking things up when finished with them. Folding clean clothes straight out of the dryer, then putting them away. But then, Lonnie would come home from work to another one of Shawna's messes. Karen made too many excuses for Shawna. That was the problem. Shawna knew how to do basic housekeeping. She was just lazy and spoiled.

Lonnie waved the annoyance away. She could well be in her few last days here, anyway, so why worry about it now. Now, for the guys' room. She'd had to switch work days this week. The old couple's daughter had had to go out of town or something. And when Lonnie had called Max from the old folks' house yesterday to tell him she'd be off today, he said he'd planned to take today off work too. But, he'd said, he had some errands to run. He didn't say what the errands were. He was being very mysterious.

She'd felt deliciously swoony at the time, and the feeling was back again now. She couldn't help but suspect that his "errands" had something to do with her. Being uncomfortably packed in here with so many people had pushed up the timeline for them, she thought, especially since it put goddamned Greta right in their faces all the time.

Now for his bedroom. Wayne and Max were reasonably neat but oh, that Oliver. Clothes, change and crumpled up tissues (ew!) lay on the floor next to his bed. Oliver and Shawna were the slob king and queen of the farmhouse. Oliver's boots were actually on the bed. Who leaves their damn dirty boots on the bed? Well, Lonnie was here to sweep and that was it. She wasn't putting a damn thing away, unless it was Max's. Wait... Where was Max's desk? Max's desk was missing.

Aha! Maybe he'd rented a place for her and himself today, and had already started moving into it. God knew she'd dropped enough hints. Well, she wouldn't ruin his surprise. She swept her way out of the bedroom and down the hallway, feeling so light she might just fly away on her broom haha!

She didn't even mind now that Greta's room was next. Greta and Emma were out. Hopefully, Greta had finally taken her lazy ass out to look for daycare and a job. Greta's bedroom was neat, at least. Lonnie gave credit where it was due.

She stubbed her pinky toe then, and it hurt like hell. Behind her hard shut eyes, she saw blooming stars. She'd stubbed her pinky toe on... Max's desk.

Pinky toes were a damn evolutionary tragedy. So tender and sticking out on the outer edge of the foot, in prime position to get injured. They should be covered in thick keratin, like a hard claw.

As the physical pain receded, emotional pain flooded in to fill the void. Max's desk was in Greta's bedroom. Max, Greta and Emma, who were all usually here at this time of day, were all out. Were they out somewhere together?

She sat on the edge of the bed. Okay, so maybe Max gave Greta the desk. Property was divvied up in a divorce, after all. And just because Max, his *estranged* wife and child were all out at the same time didn't mean they were out together.

It all came down to the chifferobe, she reasoned. If his clothes were put away in Greta's bedroom, then he'd gone back to Greta. There wouldn't be any other logical explanation, then.

First, she'd sweep. Robotically, she did, bracing herself for the grim possibility.

Then, she did it. She opened the chifferobe doors.

Inside, Greta's clothes were on right side. And Max's were on the left. Some were hung up. The rest, neatly folded and stacked.

She felt the walls waver just a bit. A tremor? She'd have to look it up, see if they were on a fault line.

In the meantime, it would be horrifying and gross to dwell on the possibility of vomiting up her own heart. She pushed the feeling firmly out of her mind.

TJ came bouncing into the room. Lonnie said, "What the fuck are you so happy about, bitch?"

TJ whooped in surprise, then doubled over, laughing.

Her laughter startled Lonnie into laughing, too. For a minute, she forgot that her life had just gone completely to shit without warning. Again. She said, "I'll be done in ten minutes."

It wasn't over yet. This might be nothing more than a momentary backslide. Of course, that wouldn't be unusual with a man who had a child to consider. A decent man would, naturally, have momentary doubts about divorce, because of his child.

It would then be up to Lonnie to decide if she'd give him another chance. No doubt Greta used the kid to make Max feel guilty. She probably found out that Max was in love with Lonnie and got jealous. She probably just wanted his paycheck anyway. She was just too lazy to get a job and used their kid to manipulate Max.

TJ and Lonnie were quiet on the ride. Lonnie was in shock about Max and TJ was probably still nervous about what that Montie chick might say to her.

They got there. Montie was very nice. She had a cute kid and a nice house. And a big-ass rock on her finger, too. Lucky bitch. Montie said, "Hi there, TJ. I was hoping I'd see you again." She stood there, stroking TJ's hair. Which wouldn't be that strange for a hairdresser to do but then TJ started stroking Montie's hair back. Lonnie thought the walls wavered for a second here, too. Was nothing as it seemed?

Montie said, "Would you two like a glass of wine? I have red or white. Or Coke? And who wants to go first?"

Lonnie had had enough for one morning and didn't feel she could take another issue that wasn't as she expected it to be. She plopped down in the client chair. "I'll go first. And a Coke would be great." She was older than TJ but TJ had already gotten to be married and have a kid. Therefore, Lonnie felt she was owed getting to go first.

TJ's nervousness was obvious. TJ had an unnatural smile pasted on her face and she kept rubbing her hands together, like she was about to pray or beg or something. TJ said, "I have to go to the car real quick."

When TJ left, Lonnie blurted, "Just shave it."

"What?"

"Shave my head, please."

Montie leaned in. She whispered, "Cancer?"

"Yes."

"Oh. I'm sorry."

"Well, that's all right." Lonnie sipped her soda, enjoying the sympathy a little bit.

Montie swiveled the chair around so Lonnie faced the large mirror on the kitchen wall. She parted Lonnie's hair down the middle and soon had one side of it shaved cleanly off. That side of Lonnie's head felt a bit cold now.

Lonnie caught her reflection in the mirror. She thought she looked edgy. LA cool. She said, "Stop there. That's good."

"What?"

"That's enough for now. Thanks. How much do I owe you?"

"Um. Well, okay. If you're sure." Montie said an amount and Lonnie paid her just as TJ returned. TJ did a double take, after she, too, caught Lonnie's reflection in the mirror. All the big owl eyes around there cracked Lonnie up. She said to TJ, "Your turn."

Montie said, "She wanted me to do that," as if she expected to be accused of shaving half Lonnie's head without permission. She told Lonnie, "Come back when you're ready to have the rest of it gone, okay? No extra charge."

TJ butted in to explain how she wanted her hair trimmed. Then she apologized for butting in. Lonnie was glad when Montie put the bib thing over TJ, covering up that weird hand wringing thing TJ kept doing.

Montie said, "Oh, that's quite all right, baby doll." She pulled a lock of TJ's hair back, and kissed TJ's exposed neck.

Lonnie went to wait in the car. She just couldn't deal with any more surprises. Well, unless she was the one doing something unexpected.

On the ride home, TJ started going on about Lonnie's hair, asking why she'd had it done that way. Lonnie turned the radio way up to drown her out, then laughed as if impressed with her own rudeness. Then she handed TJ some gas money, to sort of make up for it. She felt crazed.

As they pulled in at the farmhouse, Lonnie said, "Let's go to Ray's Ribs tonight. They have an open mic on Fridays."

"I don't know. You're not going to do anything else unusual, are you?"

"Nope. Fist bump!" Lonnie clacked her fist against TJ's limp hand, something she'd learned from Shawna. Not that TJ had any room to talk about doing unusual things.

TJ shrugged. "I'll ask my dad if I can take the car but it's probably okay."

"See you at eight."

At five minutes till eight, Max and his stinky little family still weren't home. Lonnie put on her red dress. She hung a silver bangle bracelet over her ear, on the bald side of her head. It kept falling off so she secured behind her ear with some tape. She put on some of Shawna's red-black lipstick, in front of their shared wall mirror. She thought, *Edgy, defo, bruh,* wondering if those words were still in style. She and TJ arrived at the car at the same time.

And there was Shawna, in the backseat. Already buckled in. She said, "I want to come too!"

Shawna must have heard TJ talking about going out tonight. TJ looked at Lonnie, who said, "Okay. I guess?"

TJ shrugged and started the car. If Lonnie had been thinking about it, she'd have guessed TJ wasn't in a hurry to tangle with Shawna again, seeing as how Shawna was twice TJ's size. Lonnie said, "You know, Max is the only guy I know who manages to be weird as hell and boring as fuck at the same time."

TJ and Shawna both pleasantly agreed. As a reward, Lonnie told them she considered them her very best friends. They pleasantly agreed with that, too.

At Ray's, the Friday night special was two meats and two sides, plus a dinner roll.

Lonnie got sliced donair and a sausage, with poutine and slaw. *Why not take a walk on the wild side,* she thought. Well, it was at least giving something a second chance, she figured, *and* being open to new experiences. They found a table and set their trays down. Shawna said, "Hey, half your hair is gone."

Lonnie nodded.

Shawna said, "Cool." They picked up their sausages and slapped them together in agreement.

Shawna said, "Sausage bump!" TJ laughed, and they told her that since she laughed, she had to buy a round of beer. She did.

TJ said, "Um, is that a bracelet hanging over your ear?"

"No," Lonnie said.

A middle-aged woman decked out in a tie-dye dress and headscarf with peace signs all over it, got up on the stage and recited a poem that she'd written. She enunciated each word with great emotion, waving her arm in the air. It was a rhyming poem about how Nat smashed her heart flat, splat.

Lonnie kept her gaze on her plate and paid intense attention to eating her dinner. She feared either bursting out in tears over the poem, or cracking up laughing. She didn't want to embarrass herself or hurt the poet's feelings. Especially since she was a fellow heart splattee and everything.

Next, a tall, lanky dude with a manbun played a John Prine song on his guitar. One of Lonnie's all-time favorite songs, "Clay Pigeons." She signaled the waitress for another beer, and Manbun thought she was waving at him. He nodded. Then it was like he sang the rest of the song directly to her.

TJ nudged her. "He's looking at you," she said. Lonnie already knew that because she was looking back at him. She was thinking about just plugging him in where Max had stepped out, getting engaged to Manbun instead and moving in with him.

When the song ended, some other guy got up there and started doing a magic trick.

The waitress came around with three icy mugs of beer. She said, "They're from that gentleman over there. His name's Leo."

Manbun was Leo. He waved from his table. TJ motioned him to come over.

A few acts and a few beers later, Lonnie found herself in Leo's car, on the way to his place.

"So, where do you know your two friends from?" he said.

"TJ and Shawna? Well, they're sort of friends but mostly just roommates. We're from the apartments in Nomads Nest, over the truck stop that burned up?"

"Oh, yeah. Sorry to hear that."

"Yeah. Well, now all of us, from the six apartments, are staying together in a big old farmhouse. The old Olsen place?"

"Yeah. I went to school with their grandsons."

"Small world, huh?"

"It is." He put his hand on her leg.

"How far are we going?" Lonnie couldn't believe she was going home with this guy. She didn't really do impulsive things. With the exception of hitching a ride with a trucker to another country and having half her hair shaved and everything. But before that, no.

"Just a few miles more."

"Okay. Hey, I really love that song you played. You did it just right, too. Sounded just like him."

"Thanks."

His place was a small, older mobile home in a trailer park. It's was bare-bones, but clean.

"Beer?" he called, from the kitchen.

"Sure." She thought about how nice it would be to live there. A sweet, cozy love nest, with a bit of space from any other housing units.

They started making out, pausing for sips of beer now and then.

Soon, he held his hand out to help her up, presumably to lead her into his bedroom. She said, "No. Here." It seemed more porn-ish to do it on the couch or bent over the reclining chair, or even on the living room floor. It was her first one night stand and she wanted it to be properly porn-ish.

He smiled, and sat back down. She excused herself to the restroom.

There, she discovered that her period had arrived early. With a vengeance. She couldn't even be an easy lay correctly.

She rummaged around in the cabinet under the sink and located a box of tampons. She was grateful for that, but then she wondered if their owner had left them behind or was possibly still around. Since she wouldn't be doing anything exciting that night after all, she went ahead and took a quick bath on her bottom half, a "whore bath," she thought, snickering in her drunken, pitiful state. Finally, she inserted a tampon, then wrapped her panties in toilet paper, before discarding them in the wastebasket.

When she was returning to the living room, she heard "Clay Pigeons." Leo had put it on though, he wasn't playing it himself. He'd lit a few candles, scattered on surfaces around the room. A few condoms lay on the coffee table, a neat row of little squares. She guessed the gestures might mean he really liked her.

"Um," she said, "I just got my period, so…"

He looked angry, for a moment. Then he said, "Oh. Uh, that's okay. Do you mind if I just…?" He was unbuckling his pants.

She was completely out of the mood and wanted to go home but it seemed like poor manners to say so. She said, "No, I don't mind." He took all his clothes off. She left all hers on. But she tried to be a good sport, assisting him with her hands and mouth.

After a while, he said, "I got it." He began to pleasure himself. She felt kind of offended and kind of icked out. She didn't feel like watching him beat off. It reminded her of something a baboon at the zoo would do, before flinging doo-doo at everybody. She slipped into the kitchen and grabbed another beer from his fridge, taking her time about it.

She returned just as he finished himself off. After what she thought was a respectful time interval, she said, "Hold on. I'll get a paper towel." She started back to the kitchen, where she'd seen a roll of paper towels on the counter. She wondered if she should clean him up or just hand him a paper towel or give him the whole roll. She just couldn't think tonight.

She pulled off one paper towel and approached him, guessing she should do something personal, kiss him or something. But he waved the proffered paper towel away, saying, "That's okay, I got it." Then he swiped some cum off his stomach with two fingers and… and he ate it.

He swiped again, and stuck his cum-covered fingers into his mouth again. Then, a third time, and he dared to give her what he apparently thought was a sexy look.

Lonnie took a few sips of beer and concentrated on them, fighting off the nausea that rose in her throat. She said, "Can you take me home now?" She stood by the door, with her shoes and coat back on, hand on the doorknob.

He licked his lips. "Uh, sure." He started getting dressed.

The ride home was quiet. He already knew where the old Olsen place was.

He pulled into the driveway, turned the car off. Turned to her.

She was not going to kiss him. No way. Never. Not after...

His smile dimmed. After a long moment, he said, "I'll call you?"

"Oh, I'm moving to Los Angeles. Tomorrow."

He started to say something else but she was already getting out of the car. "'Bye," she called, as she hurried towards the house. She walked around the wrap-around porch, needing a minute to brace herself for whatever she might find inside.

She trudged out into the backyard, and stood there transfixed for a while, at the fluorescent green glow in the sky, with a thin horizon of fuchsia. The Northern Lights. A reminder that there was a big world out there. She needn't be confined to any small misery.

Her glance swept downward, in time to see shadows behind a set of sheers. A man and woman embracing, Max and Greta, in Greta's bedroom. They could at least have the decency to turn off the lights. Or shut the drapes.

She hurried inside, suddenly aware that her feet were freezing in the snow.

It was dark and quiet in the farmhouse.

She got a glass of water and sat down at the pushed-together tables. She sat there for a while, letting her mind settle. She pictured herself on a journey in life as well as on a map, about to leave a small dot on the road and head for one of the largest in existence. She started keying in letters on her phone, *Live-In Help Wanted. Los Angeles, California.*

A Sad Good-Bye

The dog's barking made Fleura-Dania jump, causing the knife in her hand to slip, slashing the pumpkin's mouth. Her nerves were so jangled that, if asked, she'd estimate it would take them at least a full year to settle down, the same amount of time that she'd spent in constant turbulence with Chad. It was only Oliver coming down the steps now, though.

"Shut up," Oliver said to the blue-eyed Arctic mutt, scratching its ears. Jezebel rolled over on her back, tail wagging.

"Great," Fleura-Dania said. "All a burglar would have to do is give her any attention at all and she'd switch sides on me."

"She should know me by now anyway. She's probably stupid." He rubbed the dog's tummy. "Aren't you stupid, huh, girl?"

"Too bad she's only loyal to the one I'm the most worried about." She snickered, eliciting eyebrow raising from Oliver.

"That's funny?" he said.

She'd gotten a little gleeful there, thinking about taking the fucker's dog away. She could definitely see Chad weeping over the loss. She hoped so. "Ah, whatever," she said, getting back to cutting out the facial features she'd drawn on the pumpkin.

Oliver said, "A white pumpkin?"

"Got something against whities?"

Oliver shook his head. He called to her a minute later from the kitchen, where he was rummaging through the cabinets, "We got any more Ramen?"

"I think Gramps ate the last one. There's some canned spaghetti in there, though."

"Cool. Want some?"

"No. Thanks, though."

She finished carving the jack-o-lantern, then stood back to admire it for a minute, much needed proof to herself that she could at least do something right. "Now, where to put it? Nobody will see it down here."

"I can put it on the counter in the store, if you want."

"Okay. I don't know why I bought it anyway. It just jumped into my cart at the grocery store, I guess." She guessed she should have more important things to do but the truth of it was, she didn't know where to start.

She'd fallen off the yellow brick road good this time. Got involved with Chad the Bad until partying with him and fighting with him filled up her world, then spilled over. She got so behind in her classes that she just gave up. She had to get out anyway.

She'd dumped her useless idiot self on Gramps, completely forgetting he didn't have the apartment with the extra bedroom anymore. He and Oliver were staying in the burned truck stop's newly re-furbished basement. And now, so was she.

Gramps had moved his stuff out of the only bedroom down here, giving it to Fleura-Dania (Or "FD," as her friends called her). The same day, he'd bought and installed a locking doorknob on the bedroom door, plus an extra hook and latch lock for it, too. Oliver had wandered in and innocently asked Gramps what he was doing. In response, he received Gramps' sternest look, the one that signaled you'd better not get smart with him, if you knew what was good for you.

Oliver had backed up, hands in the air as if in surrender. Fleura-Dania, FD, didn't know if she should be amused at Gramps or afraid of Oliver, or both. Either way, she was sure to take the dog with her when she went to bed. But she soon lost any worry of Oliver trying to attack her when she slept, or any other time, for that matter. That would be more like Chad. Oliver seemed to her the type of guy who waited for women to come to him. He didn't seem conceited, though. Just laid back.

Oliver tended to the customers in the newly restored convenience store and at the fuel pumps. The apartments above it were still being re-done after the fire. She didn't know exactly why Gramps was here, though. She guessed the farmhouse was too crowded for Gramps' liking. Or maybe the truck stop's owner, who Gramps was friends with, had asked Gramps to stay here, to keep extra eyes on the place. When she'd asked Gramps about it, he just shrugged.

Gramps and Oliver really hadn't seemed to mind it, when she showed up last week, her car stuffed with all her worldly possessions and Chad's dog. Chad's former dog. Her dog, now. Chad's punishment because he'd slapped her and cheated on her. She felt so better with the big dog by her side wherever she went. She felt safe and... loved?

After the year FD had spent with Jezebel, FD couldn't bear to give her up anyway. And why should she have to? She'd been the one who took care of Jezebel, fed her and walked her twice a day. And he'd been the one who ruined their relationship. She was the one who left him but only because he made staying utterly miserable. Yep, everybody got what they deserved. She got Jezebel and Chad got to keep the disgusting STD he'd passed on to her. She couldn't even stand to think of it. Gonorrhea! Even the sound of the word was repulsive. He had no business engaging in the behavior where he got it in the first place. Why should she have to tell him she was diagnosed with it? Nope! Haha!

Gramps and Oliver both seemed like they were actually happy that she was here. Like they might be sad if she left. Well, Nomads Nest was a pretty boring place, so maybe they would be. After Chad, she was finding it a bit hard to feel like anyone would truly want her around, though. She tried to make herself useful.

Wiping her pumpkin gloppy hands on a kitchen towel, she said, "Got any more laundry? I'm ready to go to the laundromat."

"Nope, I think you got it all. You don't have to wash my clothes, though."

"No worries. I don't have anything else to do."

At the laundromat, it pleased her to watch the four loads of laundry tumble in unison, in the front load washers' soapy waters. Getting things done was satisfying, calming. She had a nice orange soda and bag of chips from the vending machines, on the table in front of her. And Jezebel stood guard between her and the door.

She got the notebook and pen out of her purse and turned her attention to the story she'd been working on. It was interesting, writing this one out instead of typing on a keyboard. She'd noticed that writing by hand seemed to engage a different part of her brain than typing on a laptop did. A more intimate or primitive part. She wrote: *Faithful dragon by her side, Taza approached the cave's entrance. She peered in cautiously, though she couldn't imagine that whatever might await her could come close to the disaster she'd just left behind. She barely set foot inside, when the dragon growled---*

"Dogs aren't allowed in here," someone said.

"Well, she's a support animal, though."

The girl who'd tried to correct her stood there looking confused. She wore a white smock, with the laundromat's name on the breast pocket, "The Scullery." A nametag was pinned on below that. It said "TJ."

FD found herself babbling because lying made her nervous, even if it was only a small and dumb lie. Of course she knew dogs weren't allowed in here. It said so right on the sign on the door. And as far as she knew, "emotional support animal" basically meant nothing, legally speaking. The law only called for exceptions for service animals, which required... Well, she didn't know what all was required. She just knew it was more than simply announcing that your pet was your emotional support animal.

She continued babbling at the attendant. "Oh, I see you go by initials, too. I go by FD. My name's really Fleura-Dania, if you can believe that. I've been called all sorts of things, though, like 'Fire Department.' Which is probably better than Fleura-Dania, when you think about it. As far as that goes, I've also been told Fleura-Dania sounds like a disease, and---"

"I don't have a name. Only the initials. I'm new here. It's my first day."

"Oh. Well. Congratulations!"

"Ha. Yeah, thanks a lot. I'm a lesbian."

FD had just taken a swig of soda, which she choked on now, caught between swallowing, gasping and laughing.

Recovering, she said, "Oh. Well. Congratulations on that too, then!"

"Thanks. What I meant to say was I'm a *new* lesbian, at the same time that I'm a new employee. I've never had a job before. Well, aside from babysitting and stuff like that. So, that's not just one big new thing but two big new things at the same time. Isn't that wild?"

"Very wild. Quite a coincidence. Or are they... now, those two things aren't related, are they?" FD realized she sounded like an idiot. Then again, the girl seemed pretty good at blurting things out herself.

"Yeah, they're related. See, me and my girlfriend are moving in together at the truck stop apartments in Nomads Nest, as soon as they're fixed. I lived there before the fire, too. I'm working here to save up for it. I also make jewelry. My website is TJewelry.com. If you want to check it out or anything. I'll give you ten percent off."

"Thanks. I'll look it up." FD was tired of the awkward conversation. She turned back to her story.

TJ didn't seem to notice that she'd been dismissed. She said, "I know your grandpa. Wayne? He lives above the truck stop, too. Lived, I mean. And will soon live there again too, probably."

"Wow. Small world, huh? I guess you know Oliver too, then?"

TJ seemed not to hear her. She walked away, and disappeared into the back room, then came back with a wash rag and spray bottle. She started wiping down the machines on the other side of the room.

Strange girl, FD thought. Oh, well. She wanted to get back to her story anyway. She wrote: A strange girl answered the dragon's growl, from deep within the cave. "I know your grandpa," she bellowed...

FD stopped at the grocery store on the way home. She already had one of Gramps' credit cards. He gave it to her for emergencies, when she'd first gone to stay in the dorms a couple of years back. He'd said she could use it for the household now. He'd be returning from a haul today and might even be home by now. She thought she'd fix a nice dinner. Pork chops sounded good. With green beans and new potatoes. She passed by some loaves of garlic bread, wrapped in foil, and grabbed one of those, too. Ooh, and she'd get a frozen, ready-to-bake apple pie for dessert.

FD didn't mind if her display of domestic skills impressed Oliver a little, too. Of course, she felt too... undone to want to deal with another guy right now. Too traumatized or dramatized or whatever you'd call her current state. But she couldn't help but be drawn to Oliver anyway. His dark, watchful eyes and easy-breezy way was appealing. He was the opposite of Chad. He was like the anti-Chad, which seemed to her, beautiful.

Back at the truck stop, she'd just started heating up the pan with a little oil for the pork chops, when her phone rang. It was someone from the hospital.

She turned the stove off, put her coat and gloves back on and rushed out to her car, Jezebel by her side. Gramps had suffered some kind of medical emergency. He wasn't doing well.

After starting the car, she pulled off a glove and called her mother, who said, "I know, sweetheart. I'm on my way now. See you at the hospital."

FD hyper-focused on driving to the hospital, and then on parking, and then on getting to the emergency department reception desk. She could hold herself together, as long as she remained in robot mode.

FD was led to a small office, where her mother was already seated, across the desk from an older man in a white jacket, who wanted FD to know that they were very sorry but. They'd done everything they could but.

Gramps was dead.

FD's mother and the man, a doctor, FD supposed, talked about what had happened. Her mother asked if his recent, recurring headaches might have been warning signs. Warning signs of... words FD didn't understand or care about. Knowing them wouldn't bring Gramps back.

"Would you like to see him?" Her mother asked.

No, she would not like to see him. she said, "I think I'll just go now. If that's okay."

"That's fine, sweetheart," her mother said, dabbing at her face with a Kleenex, her makeup impossibly smeared.

She cried all the way home. Jezebel howled in unison, on the seat next to her. *Now that's what I call a friend,* she thought.

When she walked through the door, Oliver hugged her. He already knew Gramps was gone, though she wasn't sure how. He said, "You sit down right here, dear. I'll heat up your plate."

A couple minutes later, he put a plate of pork chops, potatoes, green beans and garlic bread in front of her. He'd finished cooking while she was gone. He popped open a cold beer and set it down in front of her, too.

She wanted the beer but didn't feel like eating. She took a small bite now and then anyway, to show that she appreciated the gesture. Chad wouldn't have thought to do anything like this. Being shown care like this nearly made her start bawling all over again.

It occurred to her then that leaving the hospital so abruptly was not right. She and her mother had had a few falling outs this past year and hadn't made up from the latest one yet. Their arguments were over Chad. Her mother had been right, as usual. Trying to look out for her, as usual. And now she'd fled the hospital leaving her mother there on her own, when she'd just lost her father.

After thanking Oliver and putting the remains of her plate into the fridge, she went to her bedroom and called her mother.

Then she packed a suitcase, collected Jezebel, and drove to her mother's house, to help with Gramps' final arrangements.

#

A few days later, she was back at the truck stop basement to get her things. Going back to live at her mother's house felt like a big, depressing step backwards, in a way that staying with Gramps had not, for some reason. But without Gramps here, it would be presumptuous to stick around. She had to go.

Oliver was watching TV in the big room next to the kitchen, the one where he and Gramps had slept. Some taped up boxes were stacked by the door, with "Wayne" written on them in black marker. He'd packed up Gramps' things for her. How thoughtful. He said, "The rest of his stuff is at a storage place in Fireweed, U-Store."

"Thanks, Oliver. For everything. You didn't have to pack all that up. My mother and I already cleared out Gramps' storage unit."

He looked at her a long while, and she looked back at him. She broke away first. She didn't want him to think she was trying to play on his sympathy to get an invitation to stay here. She said, "Okay, then. If it's all right with you, I'll just go pack my stuff up now." She turned to go the few steps into the bedroom.

He called after her, "Wait, don't go. I mean, unless you want to. You're welcome to stay, though. The first level of apartments are almost ready and I was looking for a roommate. If you want. I mean, just as friends and all that."

FD liked that idea. She liked it a lot. She said, "Just as friends, right?"

"Sure."

"One more thing. And if it's not okay with you, I completely understand. As you know, I don't have an income right now. I have an inheritance coming though, from Gramps but it might take a little while before I get it. I'd be happy to sign IOUs or whatever. But, again, if not, no prob---"

"Sure. No problem. Oh, I almost forgot. Speaking of money, I think you do have some now anyway."

He opened the closet door, and rummaged around, emerging with a box. "This was Wayne's emergency stash. You know old people and their thing about cash." She opened the box. She hadn't known old people had a thing about cash but it was sure nice to get some right about now. A quick look showed that there was at least a few thousand dollars.

"Wow. Thanks," she said. She'd have to consult with her mom about it, but she knew her mom would at least let her have half of it.

He said, "You're welcome. I mean, it's yours."

"Great. Well, how much do I owe you?"

"Nothing yet. I don't have to pay to stay down here. And Jack wants more than one person on the premises anyway. So if you left, he'd just send somebody else."

"Ah, I see. Well, that sounds great. Thanks."

He said, "Oh, where's Jezebel? Did you leave her in your car?"

"Oh. No. I just… I gave her back to my ex. I hated to do it but she's really his dog. I started to feel bad, you know." She'd also told Chad he should probably get checked for an STD but of course she didn't regale Oliver with that information. Getting revenge had made her deliriously happy at first but then it just didn't anymore.

Oliver nodded. He said, "This might sound weird but you know, you kind of remind me of Wayne.

Huh. She'd never thought of that before. She said, "Well, thank you, Oliver. I'll take that as a compliment."

"It is," he said.

It had been a rough week, after a rough year. "Well roomie, guess I'll see you later, then," she said, heading for the bedroom, suddenly exhausted, though the sun was still out.

Relations

Gus emerged from the bedroom, grumpy at being awakened by kitchen noise. He squinted, though the sunlight coming in through the picture window was weak. His orange hair stood straight up at the back of his head, like a short feathered headdress. "What's all the damn banging around out here?" he groused to his girlfriend Cicely, who was also his sister, though only biologically.

"Um, fixing *your* Thanksgiving dinner, by myself, while you sleep, maybe? You're welcome, Chief Ronald McDonald. Nice of you to come greet the pilgrims!" She smirked, tight-lipped. He couldn't tell if she was smiling about her cute remark or if she was just mad. She turned the manual can opener with more force than should be necessary, around the top of the container of jellied cranberry sauce. "Hey, can you finish opening this? I'm about fed up with this cheap-ass can opener."

Gus took the can that was thrust at him. He wrangled with it for a while, finally managing to separate the top metal disc from the rest of the can. "Here you go. But you know, I thought we said were gonna be Canucks now. The Canadian Thanksgiving was last month. For your information, Howdy Doody's sister." Her hair was every bit as orange as his. Even oranger, if that was possible.

Of course, if she was Howdy Doody's sister, that made him Howdy Doody. The silliness softened their mutual snippiness. He wasn't even quite sure who Howdy Doody was, though he'd been called that plenty of times in his twenty years. Some old cartoon character, he thought.

Cicely told him again how she was getting tired of him presuming she should stop all normal activities just so he could sleep in absolute silence, in the middle of the day. That expectation seemed to her quite self-centered and lazy, she said, unless, of course, one was a small child or an elderly yud.

She waved her hand then, as if shooing away the negativity. He thought she probably didn't want to keep bickering and ruin the holiday meal, their first one together. Especially seeing as how it was so important to her, that she had ruined his sleep over it. "You know, Goo-Goo, I think this apartment is just too damn small," she said, diplomatic now. "I can't even sneeze without waking you up. Anyway, Thanksgiving dinner is ready. I thought you'd like it."

"Aww, I'm sure I will. No worries, Lee-lee." He'd stopped calling her "Sis" soon after they met. That's what everyone else called her, a logical shortening of "Cicely." But she'd said, all things considered, it just sounded wrong coming from him. But… it wasn't wrong. How could the best thing that had ever happened to him be wrong? He drew her into a close hug, turning his face to the side to spare her his nap breath.

They sat down across from each other at their newly assembled Ikea dinette set. It was a cozy sight, a pair of candles lit and their holiday plates in front of them: sliced turkey breast, mashed potatoes and gravy, stuffing, rolls. But the red and green of the cranberry sauce and green beans reminded him that Christmas was coming, a holiday that would seem even more sad and empty with only two people.

"Did anybody call?" he said, thinking of his parents and little sister in Great Falls. They'd be sitting down to Thanksgiving dinner with his grandparents and his aunts, uncles and cousins, right about now. He pictured them all being careful not to mention him at all, except maybe to add his name to the end of the customary pre-dinner prayer. "...And God bless Augustus Junior" his grandmother might say, just before everyone said "Amen," then dug into their holiday feast.

That's what his grandmother always used to say about her brother, drunko great-uncle Basil, who'd been permanently excused from the family after the Easter dinner when Gus was twelve. Uncle Basil had stood and put his finger up in the air after the pre-dinner prayer, as if he had an important announcement to make. After he had everyone's attention, a high Richter scale fart blasted out of his bottom and then he vomited all over the Easter ham, like he thought he'd go ahead and improve it with some lumpy barf gravy. It was epic.

Gus's mom thought he did it on purpose. She'd placed the ham prominently at the center of the table herself, so she was dang tootin' sure that's exactly where that ham had been. Uncle Basil would have had to lean way over the table and stretch himself out to boot, in order to vomit as he had, directly upon the Easter ham.

After that, Uncle Basil was only included in family gatherings in spirit, as an addendum to the pre-dinner prayer, "…and God bless Uncle Basil." Then he died of cirrhosis and was excused from the prayer, too. Gus wondered if they thought his alleged transgression was better or worse than Uncle Basil's legendary Easter eruptions. He wondered if anyone missed him.

Cicely said, "I don't think anybody called you. I didn't hear your phone ring."

"Well, I heard you on the phone. You were talking to that Lenny guy again," he said, scowling.

"Oh, come on Goo-Goo, please don't start on that again. You know Lenny's gay. Just think of him as… I don't know, a hairy girl or something. Okay? How's your turkey? Oh, hold on, let me get the salt and pepper."

She retrieved their new hen and rooster shaped ceramic shakers from the kitchen countertop, which was only a couple of steps from the table. "See, here's you." She held up the small ceramic rooster. "And here's Lenny and me," she added, hopping the hen shaker across the table by itself.

Gus snatched the shakers away from her. "Here's Lenny and you," he said, cheering up, putting the rooster in the position of mounting the hen.

"Nah, I think that's Lenny and you. You're the one who can't stop thinking about it." Actually, she'd had a giant, lifelong crush on Lenny. She'd been called a "fag hag" more than once at school. But what did it even matter now, when her feelings would never be returned. She wondered, though, if Gus somehow sensed it, if that's why he seemed distrustful of the friendship. Her mother had thrown that in her face too, when her feelings for Gus came out. *You just always have to have the one you can't have, don't you?*

She plucked up the rooster shaker and stuck him headfirst into her mashed potatoes. Gus, laughing, dropped the hen into his ice water.

The silliness broke the tension, again. She said, "He can be your friend, too. I mean, besides him being 100% gay, I've known him since I was like, five. It would be like in--- Hey, *you* should invite him to visit. He could come; he's got a passport. That'd put the two of you on a whole new footing, right? And then we'd have somebody besides just each other. Pretty please?"

Gus considered the proposition. "I'll tell you what. Put him on speakerphone the next time you talk to him and I might join in. I'll try to give him a chance. A small chance. For you."

She set her fork down so she could stroke his face. "Thanks, Goo. You'll like him lots. You know what he said, though? This cracked me up. I was whining again about how nobody understands our, you know, our situation. Here we're a full brother and sister in love with each other and he keeps butting in to tell me that what he's really worried about is our *age difference*. Can you believe that? Like me being two and a half years older than you trumps…"

Gus howled at the absurdity of it, revealing a strangely not-unattractive split between his two front teeth. "Yeah, well my sister said that I only think I'm in love with you but I'm really in love with myself. And you're, like, literally the female version of me."

"Well, I kind of am. You never told me that, though," she said, shaking her head at the wackiness of people, revealing the same split between her own two front teeth.

She said, "My family used to go around the table on Thanksgiving and say what we were grateful for. You want to?"

"If you start. Man, this food is great. I'm especially digging this gravy, Lee-Lee."

"Aww, thanks." She was about to add that it was only from a jar but she'd just received one of Lenny's pep talks, where he'd scolded her for putting herself down too much. She wasn't sure if that would qualify as putting herself down but decided not to say it, just in case. "Okay, most of all, a million times more than anything else, I'm grateful for you, babe. Now, you say one."

He finished swallowing a mouthful of food. "Why, thank you, my dear. I'm grateful for these fabulous rolls you made. Got any more?"

She got a couple more rolls from the counter and microwaved them for thirty seconds to warm them. Still under the influence of Lenny's pep talk, she didn't mention that they were store bought, too. "Um, anything else around here you're grateful for?"

"You, babe. Obviously. Duh."

"Well, that's better. But I mean, I'm sitting right here and just told you how grateful I am to have you in my life, and you tell me you're grateful for dinner rolls. Dinner rolls. Really?"

"Yeah, but you already know how grateful I am for you. I mean, didn't I just leave school and get cut off from my whole family just to be with you? Why do we have to spell everything out? Damn."

"Okay, okay."

His annoyance faded when he caught sight of her hair, illuminated in the candlelight as she leaned forward for the butter dish. Her adorable freckles and her flaming red hair were among the things he loved the most about her. Or they made him feel the most tender towards her, at least, if that was the same thing. She'd said she felt the same about him. They both felt very protective over the parts of each other that were most vulnerable, the things the other one had undoubtedly been picked on about the most. His sister's words flashed through his mind. *Was he actually just in love with himself?*

He shook his head, brought his mind back to the present. He said, "I think I told you I did that DNA thing the same week I turned eighteen. As soon as I could. My whole life, I was dying to know where I came from. I mean, my family was nice enough. Well, that is, before they came down on me over us getting together. But even though I didn't have any big complaints, I still never felt like I completely belonged with them, somehow. I guess they finally showed their true colors over you and me. I guess I never really belonged with them at all."

She chewed her food slowly and didn't say anything. After a while of that, he thought she might be mad again. He said, "I mean, who cares though, right. You make up for all that." *Damn, did every single word that came out of his mouth have to be about her?*

She said, "I think us meeting was fate. Just meant to be, plain and simple. See, I only did the DNA thing because my aunt gave me the kit for my birthday. Oh, yesterday, when you took your nap, I met the girls across the hall, TJ and Montie. I didn't say anything because I wanted to surprise you with my news. Are you ready?"

"Uh, I'm not sure. It probably depends on what your news is."

"Haha. Well, they might be able to get us jobs, under the table. Just odd jobs like babysitting, for them. They each have a kid. And they might know a couple of people who we could do housework or yard work for, stuff like that. They both said they'd ask around. You know, some money coming in, while we figure out how to get legal residency. Do you like that news?"

"Sure. That would be cool. Our savings won't last forever. Neither will your credit card."

"Yeah. I thought you'd like it. It would take some strain off. They were surprised we're a couple. They thought we were brother and sister. They said they'd even talked about if we were twins. Then they started laughing, after TJ said she thought we might even be identical. You know, the joke being that male and female twins can't be identical. It was funny. As far as that part of it goes. As for the rest of it, I didn't like it at all."

"Who cares what people think, babe. Screw them. Screw all of them."

"Well, I don't like people saying shit like that about us. You might not be sensitive about it but I am. Then it came out that Montie does hair for a living. That started when they were making fun of the lady who owns this place, Karen. Montie had had to talk her out of some crazy hairstyle that Karen had since, like, the eighties or something. They said she looked like a lunatic junkie. Montie said she'd dye my hair for me for just the cost of the dye. That would be better than trying to do it myself, don't you think? That would make us look a lot more different."

"No! I like your hair the way it is."

"Well, if people we don't even know can tell we're related just by looking at us, then I don't know why I even bothered leaving Helena, in the first place. I almost accidentally spilled the beans, after a couple of drinks haha. They've only been together for a couple of months too. They're lesbians. Hey, do you think gay people are more open-minded, because of all the shit they've been put through themselves? Like Lenny. He's very open-minded. TJ and Montie might be all right to trust, you know?"

"Well, hell. No, there wasn't any reason for you to leave Helena, if you're going to go around blabbing to everyone anyway. You're the one who wanted to leave! And of course it's different here. People thinking something is not nearly the same as people *knowing* something, see? All the other people we told, that was before we knew we were going to fall in love. Well, when we still thought we could fight our feelings off, at least. But now, you *know* what happens. You know better. You insisted we move to a whole other country over this. If you go and spill our business to people after all that, I swear to God, I'm going home."

"Is that a threat?" He hoped her holding her knife in the air wasn't deliberate, on her part.

He said, "No. It's a promise."

"Don't threaten me. Because I'll go right over there and knock on Montie and TJ's door and I'll tell them. I'll knock on every door and tell everybody."

"Okay. Listen, let's not fight. Hey, was that a pumpkin pie I saw in the fridge?"

"Well, I don't like having to hide who we really are. I don't like not being able to be myself, that's all."

"I know, babe. You'll… get used to it. Let's not worry about all that right now. Let's have some pie. I'll cut it, okay?"

"Okay. There's whipped cream in there, too. I want whipped cream on mine. I wonder what my parents are doing right now, and the rest of my family. Did you think of that, about yours? I don't think I ever missed a single holiday with my family, before now. No Thanksgiving, Christmas or Easter. Oh, and then there was Mother's Day and Father's Day and birthdays. I think that's it. Well, I must have missed something or other in there but I don't remember missing any."

"Hmm. I don't know if I missed any before or not. I wonder if your parents, our parents, ever thought about me, like on my birthdays or anything."

"Ha, I wouldn't know. I still don't know why they kept you a secret. Why they told everybody you were stillborn. I mean, was that really fucking necessary? It pisses me off. It's like, they caused me a fucking *trauma*. And now they act like I was the one who did something to them!"

"I get it. I don't like it but I think I get it. You know, like how a lot of girls don't want anybody to know if they got an abortion. My sister's friend got one and made her triple swear not to tell a soul."

"Ha, good job she did of that!"

"Yeah, I guess she told, huh? But it's probably the same idea. Maybe even more so, when they were married and already had a kid. People judge you harshly if you don't want your own kid. And they also judge about mental illness. You didn't understand it, really?"

"Oh, I don't know. I guess I'm still in shock. At least you always knew you were adopted. I didn't know I had a brother out there somewhere. I didn't know anything. Then they blame me when their fucking lie comes out. Well, I guess this is what they get for lying."

Her fork tapped on the plate now and then as she ate her pie. He didn't eat his. He said, "I see. So this is all a punishment for your parents, then?"

"Of course this isn't a fucking punishment for my parents. I can't take any more of this. We get along, then there's a flare up. Then we get along, then there's a flare up. Do it again and I'll... I'll piss on the turkey, boy." Her eyes gleamed.

She was clearly insane. Gus perked. "You mean like my great uncle and the Easter ham?"

"Yep. Sorta like that."

He ate his pie. She watched him eat. He said, "Do it."

"Piss on the turkey? Or what's left of it, anyway?"

"Yeah. I dare you."

"Well, I don't know. I don't care. Okay. Put it in the bathtub, then."

He picked up the pan that held the remains of the turkey. She got up from her chair. Before proceeding down the hall to the bathroom, they gazed at each other, matching amber eyes lit with excitement, matching gaps exposed between their two front teeth.

The Shays Contemplate the American Southwest

Karen and Jack sat back in their new matching reclining chairs, in front of a blazing fire after another of Greta's spaghetti dinners. It was Max's night to wash dishes, so the couple worked together, their little girl given various small tasks to keep her occupied. The dinners had become easier, with few residents remaining at the farmhouse now.

Karen said, "So, that's the last of the spaghetti noodle donations used up now. The tomato sauce is about gone, too."

"Thank god. Free food is good food but let's face it, there are more interesting meals to be had."

"Yep. Guess there is an upside to just about everything. Even freebies coming to an end."

Shawna held Nicholas above her head, playing like he was an airplane. Emma wandered in from the kitchen and begged to be an airplane, too. Shawna gently swooped Nicholas over Emma's head. She said, "Coming in for a crash landing. Take cover, Stewardess Emma!" It wasn't clear why a stewardess would be standing on the runway, but Emma squealed with excitement anyway.

"She's so good with him. Motherhood really suits her," Karen said, pleased. She'd halfway expected Shawna to push the childcare tasks on her, once the novelty wore off.

"Yeah. She seems like a grown-up now. Never thought I'd see the day," Jack said, shaking his head.

"I've been thinking, when Nicholas gets older, Shawna would make a great daycare worker. I think they have classes for that now and then."

"Could be," Jack said, nodding.

Karen and Jack had "faked it till they could make it," as the saying went. Now, when those moments came that Karen remembered the reality of their situation, and how it could all come crashing down around them at any time, she'd find herself momentarily shocked, still not quite believing the crash course they were going to be on, from here on out. They'd be looking over their shoulders for the rest of their lives.

She wondered how other people coped, others who found themselves getting away with something with high stakes, when their luck could always run out. And of course, rather than Jack and herself getting credit for taking responsibility, in the most useful way for all involved, they'd be in even deeper trouble, for taking in the child that no one else would likely want. She lowered her voice, "He's overdue for his baby shots, you know. And he still doesn't have a birth certificate. I don't know what the hell to do." She was afraid to take him to the doctor. She was afraid to apply for a birth certificate. She was afraid.

"Did someone say, 'It's time for a beer?'" Jack went to the kitchen, returned with two bottles of cold Molson beer, and handed one to Karen. He sank heavily back into his chair.

"I've got an idea," she said.

"Oh, hell. Not again." He laughed, but then peered closely at her, after taking a long, calming drink of beer.

"We'll talk later. We're late on our monthly meeting, by the way. And we didn't have one at all last month."

Jack sighed heavily. His elaborate sighs annoyed Karen. They always seemed to be directed at her, somehow. When she thought about all she'd done so Jack could continue enjoying life in the free world, his sighs really rankled her. She sighed back, mocking him. He raised his eyebrows.

"Oh, just forget it," she said. "Monthly meeting tomorrow? We can include our personal mess, er, life then, because my idea definitely has to do with the business. Among other things."

He looked a bit alarmed but Greta came in then and they turned their attention to her. She said, "Uh, just wanted to let you all know that Max and I are gonna be moving on. We're not going back to the apartments. Emma too, of course." She laughed like she'd just made a great joke.

Yeah, that was a real knee-slapper, Karen thought. She really wouldn't miss Greta. Greta had always been what they called "extra," these days. A bit too loud, a bit too opinionated, a bit too… much. But to be fair, the girl was probably just nervous. Karen imagined it wasn't fun to explain to someone that you'd be stopping a nice source of income for them, after they'd already suffered a huge loss, and that they'd have to go through the hassle of finding a replacement for you. Greta probably thought all that was true. Oh, Greta had a good heart. She was just a little rough around the edges. Who the hell wasn't. Karen made her voice pleasant. "Oh, really? Are you lovebirds heading back to the states, then?"

"I'd rather not discuss that, if you don't mind."

There it was, Greta being... Greta again. "Oh, sure. Sorry, hon. I didn't mean to pry. Thanks for telling us!"

Greta went back to the kitchen. Jack shook his head. It occurred to Karen that most of Jack's communication was non-verbal. He was quite good at it, really. Very expressive with his head shakes and nods and eyebrow raisings.

She said, "So, that'll only leave us four and TJ's parents here, then."

"And that will leave one more apartment that still needs a renter, once the top floor's done. Do you know if Antonio and Stella plan to move back into theirs place? The construction guy said all the units should be move-in ready by the beginning of February, by the way. We can place an ad now."

"Let's talk about it tomorrow. Eleven o'clock, as usual?"

Jack nodded. They held their monthly meetings at home now. Their new normal was a state of caution that might be called "paranoia," if there wasn't cause for it.

Even going out for unnecessary restaurant meals was avoided.

They watched the flames dance in the fireplace, listened to its little cracks and pops. Outside, it was hopelessly cold and white, with many weeks of Arctic gloom still to come. New hope surged through Karen, suddenly. Watching the hot fire, she envisioned a future in sunny-- and secure-- surroundings.

#

Karen sat on their bed, papers spread out in front of her. Jack came in, carrying two plates: ham and cheese sandwiches, potato chips and fruit quarters, along with two bottles of Molsons. He locked the door behind him.

"You'll never believe what I just heard," he said, causing Karen's heart to skip a beat.

"What? What?"

"Oh, hey. Nothing that bad, babe. I just ran into Antonio in the kitchen. He and Stella won't be moving back to the truck stop, either."

Karen exhaled. "Oh. Well, okay then." They ate in silence.

Afterwards, Karen stacked the empty plates neatly on the dresser. "Ready?" she said.

Jack nodded and Karen handed him a stack of computer printouts.

He said, under raised eyebrows, "Why are you showing me houses for sale in Roswell, New Mexico?"

Jack's expression made her stifle a laugh. He was always giving her one comical face or other. Sometimes,

like now, she didn't know if he was trying to be comical
with it or not. She said, "Hear me out, okay?"

He nodded in agreement, though he didn't appear very
eager about it.

She continued anyway. "Okay, so we've had some big
changes lately. And I'm thinking we could do better to be
more... comfortable with them. You know, change our
lives to better fit the changes in our lives. In general. You
follow me so far?"

"No. But I'm hearing you out."

She thought maybe she ought to get him loosened up
a little more before proceeding. "First of all, let me grab
a couple more beers."

"Now, that's always a good plan." He sat there, legs
out and back against the headboard, looking through the
stack of papers she'd printed out, shaking his head.

When she returned, he was still engrossed in the
papers. She took it as a good sign.

He accepted his beer, took a swig, then deadpanned,
"You want to move to Roswell, New Mexico."

"Yes. Actually, I do. And remember, you promised to
hear me out," she said.

"All right, then. May I ask why you want to move to
Roswell, New Mexico?" He wiped his mouth with the
back of his hand.

"For a few, interrelated reasons. The most urgent one
is that I think it would be smarter, safer, to leave the
country, before there's any record of Nicholas being here.
As I'm sure you're aware of, we can't go forever with a
baby who has no birth certificate. For starters, I'm afraid
they'll ask for it at the doctor's office. For all we know,

he might be on a list or something. And his features *are* pretty distinctive, you know."

"Or maybe he gets his baby shots, we file for a birth certificate, and nothing happens."

His stubbornness was getting infuriating. She spent hours and hours trying to improve their situation, and he just sat there and frowned. She said, "Weigh those two piles of shit against each other, Einstein, and tell me which pile seems heavier to you."

"That's not very nice."

"Sorry. But you get what I'm saying, right?"

He nodded and she went on. "Okay, I'd say our odds of not being locked up for a long, long time are better in a different country, first of all. Do you agree?"

He took another draw of his beer, then nodded, slowly, reluctantly.

"Okay, then. And I know you, hon. I understand that you really don't usually care for change, especially huge, monumental changes. But we have far more serious concerns than that right now. Correct?"

"Correct. But why there? Isn't that the place with the aliens?"

"Well, duh. Why else would I suggest Roswell? Of course we belong with the aliens. Duh! Seriously though, it doesn't *have* to be Roswell. But I have put a lot of effort into this proposal. And I do have a few logical reasons for settling on it, as my first choice."

"Such as?"

"To start with, it's far from here and in a different country, obviously. We could say Nicholas was born in the United States and get a US birth certificate. I think that would pretty much put us in the clear, as much as is humanly possible. Don't you?"

Noting his look of approval, she went on. "Okay. So, after that, I narrowed it down by states. A lot of little factors added up to put New Mexico in the lead for me. It doesn't seem as... regulated as a lot of places, or whatever you'd call it. I mean, the whole state is kind of rural and kind of poor, disjointed or whatever. It's maybe not somewhere where meticulous records would be kept, most importantly. Also maybe not somewhere that a home birth would seem too unusual. It's also not somewhere a little brown baby would stand out at all. And the cost of living isn't very high. I worked it out and we could sell the truck stop and retire, if we're careful. I might even have a buyer for truck stop. But I'm getting ahead of myself."

"How long have you been scheming up all this mess, girl?" Jack downed the rest of his beer, then looked around, as if hoping another one would magically materialize.

"I've been "scheming up this mess" since we got you-know-who, really, but just in bits and pieces. Then the fire came along and well, it all just all came together in my mind a couple of days ago. Anyway, all right, so that's all pretty much why I'd go for the state of New Mexico. Now, as you may have noticed, living in Antarctica as we do is not the most comfortable place to be for most of the year, *especially* when you're getting on in years, like we are. Therefore, I was more drawn to southern New Mexico, because they have warmer winters than northern New Mexico does. From there, well, there aren't many cities to pick from in southern New Mexico. Roswell is large enough to have a heck of a lot more than we have here and I'm ready for it. But it's not so big that you'd crawl under your bed and refuse to ever come out. Its population is about fifty thousand. So, there ya go."

Karen liked how this was going. He was listening and he wasn't saying "no." And she knew it just made damn good sense, all things considered. She rewarded herself with a couple of long draws of beer.

He said, "And who is this possible buyer?"

"You know Oliver the skunk?"

"Don't start," he said, but he chuckled.

"Okay. But I keep in touch with Oliver's cousin's wife, Rose? Yeah, you know we kind of hit it off. She's nothing like Oliver. Of course, she's not blood to him, which is a very good sign."

"They have that kind of money?" He looked surprised.

"Yeah, I think they do, surprisingly enough. I think they have enough to be able to get a business loan for the place, anyway. The business does turn a steady profit. And Rose and Eli got some kind of tribe money. Something to do with oil. Oliver is supposed to get some, too. If they allow animals to collect…"

Jack shook his head. She said, "Anyway, Rose and Eli are very interested. And they might bring Oliver in on it with them, or they might not. It's all still a big "if" right now, of course. What do you think, though? I mean, about all of it, so far?"

"Hmm. It's a lot to think about. I'm not saying no, though. Give me a day or two to chew on it."

"Okay, hon. Fair enough."

"You are something else, you know that? Give me some sugar."

Karen gave him a kiss on the lips, relieved that he was being reasonable. He wouldn't always be reasonable. Also, she felt elated by his comment. She'd always thought of herself as rather dull, a workhorse, not a racehorse. Definitely not a show horse. Being thought of as the type of person who was "something else" pleased her. The two of them drifted off for a nap together, while snow fell softly in the grey day outside.

Try, Try Again

There was a knock at the door and TJ panicked when she looked through the peephole. Oliver stood in the hallway.

She'd hoped not pressing him for child support would be enough to keep him away. And it had seemed to be, until now. She had to go begging to her parents to pick up the slack, which wasn't fun when they didn't approve of her "getting involved in homosexuality" and didn't have a problem telling her their views, every chance they got. As if they had any room to criticize how she lived, after... Well, it really pissed her off to have to deal with Oliver anyway. What the hell did he want?

She crept away from the door, Tony on her hip. Oliver was probably just having one of his stupid bouts of guilt, like he'd do sometimes towards the end of their marriage, after he'd failed to come home again. He'd be all sugary and meek the next day. She shuddered at the memory. But maybe it was partly her fault, since she never was all that attracted to him. She didn't think she even quite realized it though, until she met Montie and got jittery butterflies in her stomach whenever she heard Montie's voice. That's how it was with Montie at first, anyway.

"Who is it?" Montie boomed. She strode across the living room and, without waiting for an answer, flung the door open. Of course she did.

Oliver said, "Oh, hi. Is, um, TJ here?"

Montie was starting to remind TJ of Greta.

Oliver said, "Can we talk?"

"Sure," Montie said. That made TJ laugh, forgetting for just a second how worried she was about Oliver.

Montie didn't know that the guy standing in front of them was Oliver, of course. But she should have had the sense to notice that TJ was hiding out from the door. Should have had the sensitivity, was more like it.

It was too late now. Oliver started talking to baby Tony, "Hey there, buddy. How you doing, huh?" Tony babbled happily back at him. TJ allowed it but didn't offer to hand the baby over.

Montie, finally catching on, led her own son back into the bedroom she shared with him, and closed the door.

"You got a roommate now?"

TJ didn't answer him. He didn't need to know anything about her life. He needed to go away. Oliver was not responsible enough to have visitation rights but a family court judge might not understand that. She needed an understanding with Oliver. No child support for her, in exchange for no visitation for him.

He said, "I got some money for you. I got a settlement, a tribal oil thing."

"Thanks, but you don't have to. Really, I'm good. I was just getting ready to go out, so…"

"You don't want any money? You still mad? What's the matter? Talk to me, dear."

TJ slumped down on the sofa, settling Tony in next to her, on the side farthest from Oliver. "All right, then, I'll talk to you. I don't want you to take Tony."

Oliver looked incredulous. "Take Tony? What would I do with him, huh? I forget to take care of myself half the time."

"Bingo!"

"Bingo? Huh? What are you talking about?"

"I'm not talking about you taking him full-time. I'm talking about you taking him out of this apartment, without me. Ever."

"Oh. What, you don't trust me? Well, that's not very nice. Gee thanks. Hey, can I have a soda?"

TJ got up to get him one, rolling her eyes, taking the baby with her on the few steps to the kitchen.

She handed him a generic cola. In the can. No ice. Oliver didn't deserve any ice.

"It's been heavy on my mind, our divorce and everything. Now I can afford the child support. I want to take care of my kid. I also want to, you know, be your friend. Why not, you know?"

"To tell you the truth, I'd much rather if you just went away."

"I'm not going away." He took a sip of his soda, then stared at her with those dark eyes. She couldn't tell where the pupils ended and the irises began. It was disconcerting.

He said, "All right, I won't take him anywhere, then. I'll just come and see him here. Would that make you happy?"

"Well, Oliver. It won't be a problem. You see, I poisoned your soda. You're going to die pretty soon. Probably in a few minutes."

"Quit it. And listen, I don't want to make trouble for you. You get that? Just let me come see him for an hour a week. Any time you say. When can I come?"

"Any time? Don't you have a job? What, you got some tribe money so you just quit?"

"Sure, but my hours are more flexible now. I'm sort of just on-call, all the time now."

"Ugh. All right. Tuesday, at seven o'clock. Unless I have to work."

"You got a job now? Nice. Where you working?"

She ignored him. He finished his soda, then he quietly left. She found ten thousand dollars, just tossed on the kitchen table.

Montie came out of her bedroom to find TJ recounting the money. She shrieked, "Oh my god, look at all that money! Oh my god, you need to go find him and suck his dick right now. Never mind. I'll do it. Where is he?"

"Hush a sec. You made me lose count." TJ started over.

The kids were in the living room. Montie went to the sofa, and sat there, glowering. Probably because TJ had shushed her, even though she didn't mean it in a nasty way. She'd simply wanted to know for sure how much money was there. TJ got that dizzy, unreality feeling that came over her sometimes lately, with Montie. She tried to move past it. She said, "I know, let's celebrate. Let's bundle up the boys and go to the buffet in Fireweed. My treat."

That seemed to brighten Montie's mood. Once at the restaurant, they settled into the booth with full plates and discussed Oliver, for the hundredth time. Only this time, there was something new to discuss about Oliver for a change. Sitting across from Montie, TJ noticed anew how pretty she was. Beautiful, actually, with her green cat eyes and pillowy lips. It was easy to forget, in the dailiness of their routine. TJ guessed she didn't look at Montie too much lately.

Oliver was pretty, too. Not that there was anything wrong with liking pretty people but it occurred to TJ that both of her serious partners thus far had been better looking than her. She thought so, anyway. Maybe that was why she always seemed to get the short end of the stick. Maybe she should find someone uglier than her next time. Even coyote ugly. Or even uglier. Butt ugly, perhaps.

Montie's little boy exuberantly threw a French fry on the floor. Montie slapped his leg hard, setting him off howling. Their section of the restaurant grew silent. People had taken notice.

TJ sucked in her breath. It was a hard slap. She said, "Hey, now. That was a bit harsh."

Montie rolled her eyes. "Boys need toughening up. Yours could use some of that. He's gonna be a sissy if you keep coddling him."

TJ retorted, "A patriarchal lesbian. Groovy."

Montie pursed her lips and TJ wished she'd learn to think before she talked. TJ's smart remark wouldn't help anything. She remembered how furious Montie had been, back when TJ and Shawna got in a fight in Montie's house at the mothers' circle. Montie had acted like she simply couldn't tolerate any violence. Ha.

Montie said, gesturing at her son, "Watch him." She sauntered back to the buffet, like the queen of the world. She was frigging bossy. What TJ would have said to her would be, *"Can* you watch him?" A request, not an order. Montie gave orders but she sure didn't take the slightest hint of an order herself. Just look how sulky Montie had been only an hour ago, when TJ had shushed her so she could re-count the money.

TJ redirected her thoughts to the nice chunk of cash she'd just gotten. She wanted to have a good evening. There'd been few enough of those lately, without her ruining another one with her negativity. She thought about investing some of the money in her jewelry business. Now she could try some real silver and semi-precious beads. She could also replenish her secret stash, which was just about wiped out now.

Montie returned, plate piled high with mashed potatoes. TJ brought up the first conversation topic that came to her mind, wanting to keep things nice. She said, "Speaking of divorces, how's yours coming along?"

"Oh, he's still doing that thing where he alternates between threatening me and trying to get me back."

TJ had come to suspect that Montie encouraged the part where Fred tried to get her back. In spite of Montie's complaints, it seemed to TJ that Montie liked the attention. Montie definitely missed her nice house, her plushy lifestyle. TJ was certain of that, since Montie said so all the time.

"Do you ever think about going back to him?" *There. She'd said it.* Lately, she sort of wished Montie would. Moving in together so soon had turned out to be a lot. They hadn't known each other as well as TJ had thought. TJ hadn't known what a mean side Montie had. And with two pending divorces and two kids in a small apartment, the stress took a toll.

Montie said, "I don't know. I mean, no. Hell no. Oh my god, I can't believe I forgot to tell you. You have to swear not to tell anybody, though. I mean cross your heart and hope to die. Cicely will *kill* me if she finds out I told anybody. Swear!"

TJ said, "Okay, I swear not to tell. Here, let me get these guys situated first." The boys were finished eating, so TJ directed them under the booth, with a couple of toys from her diaper bag. It was probably tacky to let kids out of their seats but it was just a cheap-o buffet anyway, whatever. She said, "Look, you guys! Your own fort."

"Okay," Montie primped, as if about to be interviewed on the evening news or something. Before speaking, she refreshed her lipstick, combed her hair with her fingers. She said, "You know how we could have sworn that Cicely and Gus were twins?"

"Yeah?"

"Well, girl. Good thing you're sitting down. So, Cicely came over for a cut and color while you were at work. We started chatting and drinking wine and stuff and she tells me that the reason she wants the brown hair color is because she and Gus looked too much alike, with that red hair. I said, yeah, when TJ and I first saw you two, we thought you were twins. You know, like we told her before."

"Uh-huh."

"Well, then the truth came out. She just blurted it out all of a sudden, girl. They aren't twins. But they *are* brother and sister."

"What the fuck! No way!"

"Yes. I'm afraid so," Montie said, triumphantly. "They only met each other a few months ago, though."

"So, they're half siblings, then?"

"Nope. Full-blooded brother and sister. The parents already had Cicely when her mom got pregnant again. But she didn't want another one."

"Well, that's weird."

"Yeah. Well, the mother was suicidal. She couldn't handle another one. So when Gus was born, they adopted him out. Cicely and Gus found each other accidentally, on one of those DNA sites Cicely didn't even know he existed. So, then they met in person and then they fell in love."

Driving home, TJ was still trying to sort out that strangeness in her mind, about Cicely and Gus. She couldn't decide if it was disgusting or really kind of beautifully, tragically romantic. Montie snapped, "Watch the road, dumbass."

Dumbass? TJ told herself to just give Montie a minute. TJ's driving had just scared Montie. She'd apologize for saying that, in a minute.

Montie didn't apologize, though. She started talking about how Cicely also wanted to get her teeth fixed, because the crookedness of her teeth was the same as the crookedness of her brother's teeth.

Who the hell did Montie think she was, anyway? TJ said, "Back up a sec, that name you just called me. You don't talk to me like that. You can *ask* me, *nicely* for anything. But you don't *tell* me shit."

When TJ stopped at the stop sign, the blow came, to the side of her face. She'd half expected it, since it wasn't the first time. But now, she'd had enough. She slapped Montie back, clipped her in the ear, yelling that she wished Montie would just frigging die.

They shouted back and forth the rest of the way home, kids wailing in the back seat.

#

The next night, on her way home from her shift at the laundromat, TJ was thinking about the best way to end it with Montie. TJ's parents had just moved into a house in Calgary, a nice three bedroom with two bathrooms and a small yard for Oodle, who had been sent to them. Poor Bruce. TJ pictured him taking Oodle to the pet shippers for her mom, and selling her mom's house for her, too. He was so good. It seemed cruel to TJ that her mom made him wrap up her old life for her, after dumping him to go back to TJ's dad.

As for herself, at this point, living with her parents again seemed a lot better than continuing to live with Montie. Her parents had bought her a car and gave her money every month as it was, so she doubted they'd even ask her for any rent. She could stay there for a while, save up her money and plan for her future. As the saying went, three's a charm. She hoped her third try at adulting would at least be better than her other two tries had been.

"Hey, baby," Montie greeted her at the door with a big smile. Her hair and face were done and TJ had to admit she looked like a million bucks. The kids had already been put to bed and a pan of lasagna was in the oven. Coming in from the bitter cold night, the place was so welcoming, warm, candles burning on the table, fragrant with oregano and garlic. It confused TJ a bit. She wasn't expecting to walk into such utter loveliness.

Montie said, "Oh, and baby, I printed out some stuff about the rules for fair fighting. I thought we could go over it after we eat."

TJ supposed maybe they could. It wouldn't mean she couldn't still break things off if she wanted to. It wouldn't hurt to learn something new.

\#

TJ's phone rang. It was right there on the sink vanity but she didn't answer it. Her hands were wet and soapy; she was busy giving the boys their bath.

A minute after it stopped ringing, Montie's phone rang. So TJ wasn't surprised when Montie came in, telling her she had a call from Greta. TJ had stupidly given Greta Montie's number when Greta had asked her for it. But TJ could use the money from watching Emma, so she hadn't wanted to tell her no, and risk pissing her off. Goddamn Greta.

"Ask her what she wants," TJ said.

"Here. She's on speakerphone."

"TJ," Greta said. "Can you keep Emma overnight on Friday? This accounting course is kicking my butt. I really need a break, and it's our anniversary."

"You want me to keep her here, at my place?"

"Yeah, we want to stay over at a hotel in Calgary, so it's on the way."

Greta and Max had bought a house somewhere even farther out in the middle of nowhere. TJ wondered why, but she didn't wonder enough to ask. She said, "Okay, sure. What time are you coming?"

"Perfect. Six thirty?"

"Great. I've got to run but I'll see you then." Montie and TJ each toweled off their own son, then carried them to their respective bedrooms. When they'd moved in, they'd decided to keep separate bedrooms, each with their own son. Montie wanted to keep up the appearance of being platonic roommates, just in case her parents and jealousy prone husband ever stopped by.

After TJ got baby Tony down for the night, she went to the kitchen to wash up the supper dishes. From behind her, she heard, "That was really fucking nice." She turned to see Montie's red face, clenched lips.

TJ said, "What?"

"You'll just have some kid over here for the night, will you. Without even *thinking* to ask me. Huh, bitch?"

TJ wasn't interested in appeasing Montie anymore. Whatever lunatic spell she'd been under had broken.

What she was interested in was getting rid of Montie. She silently marveled that Montie's husband wanted her back. Maybe Montie was different with him though, who knew.

"Oh, I'm sorry," she said, though she wasn't sorry at all. "Oh wait, I think I hear Tony. I'll be right back, honey."

Montie grabbed her wrist but then let it go. "You better be right back," she said.

TJ went into her bedroom. She locked the door, then pushed her dresser in front of it. Montie's red, mad face had disgusted her. She didn't want to stay here one more night, or even one more hour. She dialed the RCMP and kept her voice low. "Hello, I need an officer here so I can leave a domestic situation safely," she began.

Montie banged on the bedroom door. "Get out here, bitch. I'm not done with you."

Tony cried. TJ picked him up. The knocking stopped. TJ guessed Montie was satisfied for the moment, after waking up TJ's kid, causing a hassle for her.

A few minutes later, there was a knock at the door. She heard Montie's voice, talking to the officer, surprised.

Someone knocked on her bedroom door. A woman's voice said, "Hello? RCMP. Open the door, please."

She opened the door. The officer came in and waited while she gathered up a few things. Coming out with the officer, she saw that Montie's bedroom door was shut. The officer said, "There's another officer in there with her. We'll keep her there until you're gone." She walked TJ out, carrying TJ's tote bag full of clothes. TJ carried her usual accessories, baby Tony and his big diaper bag. The night was frozen, the stars large.

She thanked the officer and headed for her parents'
house, after calling to let them know she was on the way.

She called Greta in the morning and told her she'd be
staying with her parents in Calgary, and could they bring
Emma there instead of to Nomads Nest. She didn't tell
Greta why.

The following afternoon, TJ's dad called, from her
apartment above the truck stop. He'd gone there to get the
rest of her things. He said Montie's bedroom was empty.
So were the living room and kitchen. Montie had moved
out already, and taken just about everything. Montie's
husband probably happily zoomed right over in his van
and packed it all up. TJ didn't care. Most of the stuff
belonged to Montie anyway. She and her mom made
gingerbread man cookies while baby Tony and Oodle
napped together, on a blanket on the living room carpet.
She pictured her dad at her apartment, taking apart baby
Tony's crib with his screwdriver, whistling as he worked.

Fireweed

Sabrina Rossi was just fucking stuck. Those were the words that most accurately described her condition, *just fucking stuck*. Well, she supposed her condition might also qualify as depression. Or failure to transition to adulthood, which was briefly covered in her college psychology class, the only class she didn't drop last semester. But, if you asked her, those were really only synonyms for "just fucking stuck."

So, when Fleura-Dania "FD" Wilson invited Sabrina to move up to Canada and be her roommate, Sabrina couldn't pack fast enough. She felt the first glimmer of hope she recalled having in quite a long time. She loaded up her old car, filled the gas tank and headed out of Spokane before her parents and brother got home from work. She texted on the family thread, *Went to stay with a friend. Will call soon.* She didn't plan to call all that soon.

She'd met FD on an online creative writing forum, a few years ago now. They'd clicked right away, becoming

critique partners, then phone friends. FD really got
Sabrina, in a way no one else did. Certainly not Sabrina's
father, who chided her daily, most recently demanding to
know what she'd done all day long then, if she hadn't
looked for a job. Her mother's thing was imploring her
just as frequently, to at least try the Weight Watchers
meetings, honey, for her health, if nothing else. Her
parents were right, of course. But it felt all wrong to her.

Three hours later, she was at the Canadian border. The
guard took a long time inspecting her passport, talking
about how little time she had left on it. She hadn't even
thought about that. Her family had all gotten passports
years ago, for a vacation in Banff. She hadn't thought of
it since then, until FD's invitation. Now she feared she'd
be made to turn around and go home, after her big text
announcement, another humiliating defeat. When finally
allowed into Canada, she was still so shaken that she
stopped for the night, at the first motel she saw from the
highway.

The next morning, she woke to a flood of texts on the
family thread. They progressed through time from
curiosity, to anger and finally, worry. But Sabrina had had
enough of family for the time being. She blocked them
all, then texted FD. She still needed a shower and
breakfast, and then she had five more hours to drive.

She drove along, in a good mood, which had become
rare for her. She felt tentatively hopeful under the big
open prairie sky, rock music playing. It was mid-April but
pockets of snow still dotted the landscape here and there.

About halfway through her journey, she stopped along
with the other cars, wondering what in the world was

going on. Her question was soon answered, when a large moose ambled into view. He seemed to her twice the size of a horse. That rack of antlers, those long, astonishing thin legs. It was surprising that he didn't collapse on them, under his own huge bulk. My goodness, she thought, look at all I've been missing. Feeling tired had become her usual state, tired and lying in her darkened bedroom, watching TV, reading novels, eating whatever food was easy to grab and eat lying down. But she didn't feel tired now.

Finally, she reached the sign that said, *Nomads Nest, Population: 12*. Population: 12? Well, that was simply ludicrous, she thought, delighted. No doubt, this was going to be an adventure. She'd have to talk to FD about collaborating on a story collection, with all the stories set right here in Nomads Nest.

She pulled into the truck stop parking lot and was treated to another wildlife sighting. Eight or ten large bunnies hopped about in the grass, at the far end of the lot. Arctic hares, she believed they were, mottled white and brown as they shed their winter camouflage.

She stepped out of the car, into cool, mint-scented wind. Someone must be growing mint nearby, likely commercially, from the strong fragrance of it. FD rushed out of the building to greet Sabrina, hugs and squeals in the invigorating breeze. It was odd to finally connect solid flesh with the voice and mind she'd come to know so well by phone. She'd seen photos of FD but still pictured her as being somehow darker, and taller.

They each picked up all they could carry from her car and started toward the building with it. "What are all those gorgeous wildflowers?" Sabrina said, nodding at the showy display of tall stalks everywhere, covered in tiny lavender blossoms.

FD said, "Oh, that's fireweed. I just learned about it myself. It's called that because it comes up after a fire. I'm sure you remember me telling you how this place burned half down. Let's see, if I remember correctly, fireweed flourishes in "disturbed environments." And it symbolizes hope and resilience."

"Fireweed, huh? Interesting. Sounds like us, doesn't it? Well, that's what I want to sound like, anyway." She laughed, nervously, thinking that "resilience" might not describe her at all.

But FD nodded. She said, "Yup. It definitely sounds like us. Oh, right this way. We have to go through the convenience store to get to the apartments upstairs. And this is Oliver, my former roomie and one of the new owners here. Oliver, this is Sabrina Rossi."

"Nice to meet you," she said. Oliver called into the back room, "Rose, Eli." A heavyset Native couple came out. Oliver said, "Thought I'd introduce you to our latest resident while we've got her right here. This is Sabrina Rossi, from Spokane, I believe? Yes. FD's new roomie. Sabrina, these are my cousins and my co-owners here, Eli and Rose Falcon."

"Nice to meet you," Rose said. "Welcome," Eli said.

FD's apartment was on the top floor, two bedrooms and one bathroom. FD said, "The building is mostly empty right now, so I pretty much got my pick of apartments. I like the view up here. Hope you don't mind all the stairs."

"Not at all. I like the extra built-in extra exercise. Now, what's this you said about changing your major? I was thinking about that on the drive. That doesn't sound like the FD I know, girl."

"Yeah, well, Gramps' death made me think. He always wanted me to pick a more practical major, so I'd have a solid income if my writing didn't work out, financially speaking. He was an artist, you know. Got his degree in Art and ended up having to drive a truck for forty years. Even though his art was, well, I think it was just amazing, and he put out a lot of it, too. His work is still in a few exclusive galleries. Anyway, when I learned how much money he'd left me, I started thinking about all he must have had to sacrifice to end up with that much money, on a truckdriver's salary. That's four whole decades of driving a gigantic truck, out on the road alone. It sounds pretty shitty to me. He did it for us. So it's to honor him."

"Ah, I see. So you're going into nursing as a kind of... tribute to your grandfather?"

"Yeah. You could say that. Plus, really, he probably has a point. It's time to grow up, maybe. You know?"

"Wow. Maybe I should think about that too, then. I mean, it *would* be nice to feel like I'll be able to actually make a decent living, at some point."

"Maybe. I mean, neither of us have that far to go, before we could have our degrees and be able to get on with it. Only a couple more semesters, give or take, right?"

"Yep. That all makes sense. And I guess being able to get out there in the real world is a lot closer of a reach than it seems, really."

"It is. Don't worry though, girl. We'll still write. We'll always write. Oh, look." Oliver, Rose and Eli lumbered in, all three loaded down with the remainder of Sabrina's belongings.

This kindness from strangers touched Sabrina. She thought it was definitely a good omen. She felt like she'd finally broken a losing streak here. Like now she had a fresh, mint-scented chance to start over, to exist as something more than a disappointment to those around her. Well, she still had some hurdles to clear, starting with finding a way to be able to legally stay here for more than six months at a time. She hoped she'd be able to step into a new, upgraded role, to get unstuck at last.

She said, "Oh, thanks so much, you all. You didn't have to do that!" As she reached to take a stack of clothes from Oliver, she felt an odd sensation, like a small critter skittering up her arm. She shivered, and looked her arm up and down. But she couldn't see the tulpa, she could only perceive it.

The End

If you enjoyed this novel-in-stories, a review at your point of purchase would be most appreciated.